Double Act

Bangkok Silom International
School Series – Book 1

JAKE LEE

ISBN: 978-1-7393267-0-8

DEDICATION

This book is dedicated to all those young people like Danai, whether you have Danai's self-assuredness or not. We are all on our own journeys.

ONE

"Where's your brother?" Danai's mother shouted up the stairs to her sixteen-year-old son. Danai lay back on his bed trying to catch up on the day's Instagram stories. "Mum! I told you. I don't know."

His brother, Beer, tended to come and go as he pleased these days. He was nineteen, at university, and figured he didn't need to answer to anyone. It irritated their mother though, as today he had said he'd be home for dinner. Danai strolled down the stairs to join her.

"The chicken can go to the dog then!" She laughed.

"Yes! Do it! Go, Mum!" Danai shouted back. It may have been a bit cruel of him to take such delight in this. He got on well with his brother these days. The three-year age gap had been a much bigger deal when Danai was younger. Now he could almost consider Beer as a friend.

The Instagram stories had a familiar tone. Some

were joyous, celebrating the last few days of the summer holiday. Others were depressingly counting down the days until school would start again.

Danai's only addition to his story that day was simple; a picture of a history textbook over which he had typed "FUCK!" and a picture of a cartoon figure with his head in his hands.

His friends knew what it meant. Their history teacher had set some background reading over the summer for the students who were continuing to study history in Grade 11. Something about World War II. All part of a campaign to get them to realise they'd now be studying history at a higher level and they needed to show real passion and commitment.

When he got to Tee's story his heart skipped a beat, or more than one beat. It began to race. "Oh, my god," he whispered to himself.

Tee was at the beach near Rayong for the last few days of summer, and Danai was very happy about it. He got to gawp at a string of photos of Tee's beautiful smiling face and beach body. His hair was ruffled, un-styled and yet perfect. Those deep brown eyes. Danai held his finger on the screen to pause the photo. He stared longingly into those warm eyes. He was lost. Lost in love. Lost in lust. Unrequited, unspoken, love.

"You are so fucking hot, Tee." He longed to be brave enough to tell Tee this to his face. Tee had a girlfriend, didn't they always? But he still wanted him to know. She surely didn't feel the same way as Danai. The final picture nearly had him rushing to the bathroom. He certainly felt an instant reaction between his legs, and it felt good. There was Tee, on the beach, in a pair of stylish, brightly, multi-coloured swimming shorts, smiling. His body was perfect. Smooth, with just visible abs. Abs that said, 'natural Adonis' rather than, 'hours in the gym'.

"You're perfect." He gently rubbed himself and daydreamed. He was interrupted by a message alert on his phone.

Fuck that reading. It's BS. No one do dat.

It was his best friend, Noom. They'd been friends since they both started at Bangkok Silom International School as eleven-year-old newbies.

He felt too lazy to type a reply so he made a video call back.

"Yo! My boy Danai!" Noom always spoke like this, a result of too much time spent watching American TV.

"You back in Bangkok now or still in Phuket?" Danai asked.

"Does this look like Phuket?" He scanned the camera around his bedroom. "My Bangkok homies need me back in town!"

"Noom, what the fuck have you done to your hair?"

Noom was always up to something outrageous. This time it was a couple of streaks in his otherwise jet-black hair. One blonde, one a sort of purply-pink.

"Come on. Tell me it don't look fine. Tell me I'm not the sexiest thing you've seen today."

"You're not the sexiest thing I've seen today."

Not even close. Mmmmmm Tee baby.

"Shit, man! Where you been today?" They both laughed. They were a classic double act, they made each other laugh. Most of the time with jokes that no one else found funny or even understood. They often referred to themselves as 'Danoom' since you'd rarely see one without the other. They came as a pair.

"Three more days only. Why's it gone so fast, dude?" Danai actually enjoyed school once he got going. The real dread was having to get back into the routine of waking up early.

"A lot can happen in three days. Coming to Siam tomorrow?"

"Why? What's happening? No one tells me anything."

"Danai, my man. Why you not down with my peeps? I'm telling you now, bruh."

"Just speak English, or Thai, or Tinglish, just not whatever this shit is!"

"OK. OK. Chill, dude. A few of us just gonna hang out at MBK. Maybe see a movie. Whatevs."

"Yeah, I'm in."

"Yeah, you're in! I gotta fly, dude!" They both slipped back into hysterics before Danai ended the call with the sort of insult one could reserve for their closest friends, "You're such a fucking moron!"

He went downstairs where his mum was watching TV and drinking a glass of wine.

"Done your history work, sweetie?"

"How do you know about that?"

She held up her phone. "Instagram."

He'd put that on the wrong profile, usually he'd put that kind of thing on his second profile which was only for friends. His other profile included family and other random people.

"Where's Dad?" he asked for no other reason than not to have to talk to his mum about his social media profiles.

"On the way home. He had a late meeting." Danai's phone buzzed with a text from his brother.

Forget dinner. Eating with friends. Tell Mum I'm back late.

"Oh, Beer will be back late."

"I just asked you where he was."

"And I didn't know then. He literally just texted me."

Why were parents so illogical? Wasn't it obvious that he'd only just received the information?

He sat down and decided to watch TV with his mum for a bit. It was a boring Netflix drama that she loved.

They were a typical middle-class Thai family. Both parents had good jobs. His dad, Wut, was a lawyer and mum, Lin, was an executive for a pharmaceutical company. Their two sons were both educated at the international school, at great cost. They were proud of their bilingualism and they spoke as much English at home as Thai.

Danai could slip effortlessly from one language to another but tended to speak English with most people at school as not all of them were fluent Thai speakers.

"Is Noom back from Phuket?"

"Yeah, I'm seeing him tomorrow."

"Oh, that's nice. How's his mum?"

"Er. Fine. I guess. I'm sure she is."

"You didn't ask did you?" She said shaking her

head. She knew he hadn't, of course. Sixteen-year-old boys tended not to ask about the well-being of their friends' parents. Noom's parents had recently had a slightly messy divorce.

"Such a nice lad Noom. He's welcome to come for dinner any time."

Danai laughed. "Yeah, I know. He's got you all fooled that boy!"

Noom was one of those guys who was irritatingly polite with all his friends' parents and as a result they all adored him.

He went back up to his room and looked again at Tee's latest photos. He spent way too long deciding what message to send. He kept typing something then deleting. In the end he opted for something safe, perhaps a bit lame.

Looking good, Tee!

In Danai's mind it was a little bit flirtatious. Flirting was an art form, and he was definitely no artist. To his delight, Tee replied within a minute.

You too buddy! Stop reading that history book!

Danai smiled. A double win, not only did Tee reply immediately but he had taken notice of his Instagram post.

Maybe he loves me after all!

Danai laughed at his crazily optimistic deduction.

Tee was one of the first friends Danai made on joining BSIS. Tee, being one of the nicest boys in Grade 6, was assigned as a 'buddy' to the shy new boy. For Danai, it was love at first sight. Though as an eleven-year-old he didn't realise it. He just thought Tee was really cool and they became friends, Danai quickly becoming part of Tee's social group.

Tee was one of those people who was good at everything, but was genuinely so modest that no one begrudged him any of his success. He often helped Danai with schoolwork, especially biology and English. It was only maths where Danai was better than Tee and occasionally returned the favour. He would never forget the feeling he had when Tee first asked for some help with the maths homework. He felt amazing. What Tee said was 'can I come over tonight to do that maths work?' What Danai heard was 'Danai, I wanna spend time with you, baby!'

When you back from Rayong?

Danai wanted to keep the conversation going.

Back already, those photos were two days ago, fake news! Ha-ha.

They exchanged a few more messages and Tee confirmed he was part of the gang going to the movies. It increased Danai's excitement for what was a pretty standard activity – hanging out in a shopping mall. He hadn't seen Tee during the last four weeks of the school break and just longed to be in his company, to see his smile, to smell his cologne. He got himself to sleep that night by thinking of Tee and imagining being with him. He hugged his pillow, pretending the object of his affection was lying with him.

Beem and Golf were almost as much of a double act as Danai and Noom. They'd been friends literally since birth. Their mothers were close friends. They'd both started at BSIS at the age of five and so were part of a rare group who would spend their entire school life at the same school. From Kindergarten to Grade 12. They knew pretty much everything there was to know about each other. They spent so much time together, often their families holidayed together. They were so connected that they regularly had the same thoughts at the same time. It was so commonplace that they'd both stopped saying, "I was just about to say that" as it was getting boring.

Beem lay back on his bed, while Golf lounged in the armchair on the other side of the bedroom. They were both glued to their phones, occasionally making random comments. Golf was in charge of the music play list, with his phone hooked up to the Bluetooth speaker.

Beem's walls were adorned with pictures both of his favourite K-Pop bands as well as some of his favourite golfers. He tried to claim that it was Korean girls he was fond of more than Korean pop, but he'd happily sing or attempt to dance to the music. He'd been playing golf since the age of six and his dream was to become a pro golfer. Of all the photos in his room his prized possession was not the happy family pictures but the one of a grinning twelve-year-old Beem with Thongchai Jaidee, Thailand's top golfer at that time. Beem was so excited when Jaidee had walked by and applauded his chip shot, and then the

Thai star waited to see Beem hole the putt and congratulated him. His friends had heard the story hundreds of times.

"For fuck's sake, Golf, stop changing the songs!"

"Gotta get the vibe right."

Golf was renowned for listening to about one minute of a song and then changing. It infuriated everyone.

"Hold everything! Here we go!" Golf screamed in excitement. His best friend didn't respond.

"Dude. I'm serious!"

"What the actual fuck?" Beem had a short temper and was often pretty moody, the classic brooding teen. His friends loved him for it.

"Yes, it might be just that. An actual fuck!"

"You're sick." After a short pause, Beem became curious. "OK. What is it?"

"I got a Line message from Nice!"

"Nice? Who's that?"

"The girl I met on holiday in Chiang Mai!"

"What? She was real?" Beem laughed at his own joke.

"She wants me, she loves me, she must."

"Why? What did she say?"

Golf sheepishly responded, "It's not so much about what she actually said…"

Beem was enjoying this. "Oh, my god, this is tragic. What. Did. She. Say?"

"She said…hey, you!" Golf made a heart shape with his hands and thumped his chest theatrically.

"Oh, fuck me, man. If that's proof of love then I've got about twenty in love with me!" His laughing intensified and he hurled a pillow across the room, hitting his mate square on the head. Golf returned it with extra force and joined his buddy in laughter. He jumped on the bed showing Beem a photo of Nice. "Tell me those eyes don't scream I love Golf!"

"Yeah, but I love golf too. Where does she play?"

"You're so fucking funny, Beemer." He glanced at the famous photo of Thongchai and sarcastically asked "Is that when Thongchai clapped your putt? Why don't you ever tell us the story?"

Beem mock-punched him on the arm.

"Dude, did you see Tee's Instagram photos today? Unreal"

"Yeah, I saw 'em. That guy. It's incredible! He is so fucking beautiful I could go gay for him."

"You? Oh, Golf, Tee is so far out of your league!"

"Nice is as beautiful as Tee." He showed Beem the photo again.

"Not. Even. Close."

"That guy." Golf was flicking through Tee's photos.

Beem nodded in agreement.

TWO

Danai woke up earlier than usual, such was his excitement at spending some time with Tee, for the first time in so long. He felt a bit embarrassed about how excited he was, and guessed this was what love felt like. Being at the same school as Tee and being in the same core friendship group meant he saw him five days a week, at least. That wasn't enough for Danai though. The lengths he would go to, just to get a glimpse of his crush were ridiculous. He knew Tee would often go to the Siam Paragon shopping mall with his mother or with his girlfriend, Fern, and so Danai often went there himself hoping to bump into him. On more than one occasion he had used Tee's updates on Snapchat or Instagram to effectively stalk him, though not in a creepy way.

He checked his phone, and saw a stream of messages from his friend Nutt that had been sent after midnight when Danai had already fallen asleep.

You going MBK tomorrow?

What time we meeting?
Danai? U there?
Guess u sleep. Txt me tmrw. Laterz.

Danai smiled, classic Nutt. A nerdy attempt to be cool. He looked at his watch and decided it was still too early to reply to Nutt, since he had texted so late. He then figured that surely his phone would have been on silent if he was still asleep so he replied anyway.

Yeah, meet at MBK like 11:30. Cya.

Within a minute Nutt had replied.

Fuck, dude, you woke me. See ya later.

Danai thought better of sending an apologetic reply in the hope that his friend would sleep again. Nutt was one of the quieter ones of their group, he often would just blend into the background but he was always there whenever anything major happened. He didn't say a lot, but he smiled and laughed a lot. Shy and dependable and a bit nerdy. Nutt was more preoccupied with schoolwork than anything else, wanting to make sure he got the grades to go to medical school and follow in both his parents' footsteps and become a doctor. He wasn't really interested in sports and didn't appear to care much about music, to the extent that when he knew a song or a band everyone was surprised.

'Come on even Nutt knows them' was a common putdown within their gang. Nutt was just one of those guys you could rely on, never any drama, everyone liked him, but no one would quite be able to pinpoint why. It was the nature of the friends; they were all different and that was just that. Nutt was Nutt.

Nutt did manage to get back to sleep for a bit, but at around nine he decided to get up and go downstairs. He waited enough time to ensure he wasn't embarrassed by a tent forming in his boxer shorts.

He stumbled into the kitchen in a half-awake state.

"Morning sleepy, it's early for you on a Saturday." His mother sat at the kitchen table eating some breakfast. "Dad's gone for a run; you just missed him you could have joined." She laughed, knowing her son had absolutely no interest in going running with his dad.

"Huh?"

"He lives! Good morning to you too."

"Morning." Nutt tried not to grunt back at her, but he wasn't properly awake yet. He poured himself a glass of water from the fridge and sat down to help himself to the platter of fruit that his mother had put on the table.

She knew after he'd eaten a bit he'd start to be more responsive so she waited a few minutes before trying to start a real conversation.

"What have you got planned today?"

"Just seeing the guys at MBK?" He munched on some pineapple.

"Oh, nice. Which guys?"

"Dunno." He hated it when his mother started grilling him about his social life.

"You don't know?"

"Danai, Tee, Beem, usual."

"Have you got any work to do for school on Monday?" She asked, trying to sound off-hand but Nutt knew this was what she was really wanting to find out.

"It's the first day of the school year! I didn't have any work to do."

"There's always stuff to do." Without thinking she cleaned up some of the pineapple drips from the table around his plate.

"I know, I know. I've done quite a bit of background reading."

"Good plan." She gave him a hug and a kiss on the cheek before getting some money out of her wallet. "Enjoy yourself today, hard work starts on Monday."

"Thanks, Mum."

She left him in peace, and he felt more relaxed. His parents were intense. They were good parents. They loved him more than anything, and he knew that. They'd do anything for him, but they could be seriously overbearing at times. School and exams, and planning for medical school was stressful enough without his parents putting him under added pressure.

Meet at your place?

It was the norm for Danai to swing by Nutt's if they were going out together, as it was on the way to the Skytrain station.

Yeah, ten am.

Danai was just getting himself dressed when Beer walked into his room.

"Don't you ever knock? I could have been naked."

"Where you going today?" Beer ignored his little brother's complaints.

"Just to MBK with the boys."

"Nice one. How's Noom?"

"He's cool, same as ever. Why you wanna know about Noom?"

"I don't, I wanna know how is sister is doing."

Danai laughed. "Come on, Beer, she's two years older than you."

"She may like a toy boy." Beer smiled. "I saw her last night, she's hot."

"I'll tell Noom, he'll be pleased to hear that." Beer ignored the heavy sarcasm.

"Just tell him, to subtly let her know how cool I am, or how rich I am, or whatever works!"

"Yeah I'll tell him, but I don't think she dates guys based on his recommendation!"

"Thanks, little bro, that shirt looks cool by the way." Beer strutted out the room, leaving Danai a bit perplexed. It was so unlike his brother to be that complimentary about his fashion sense. It felt good to get Beer's approval. If there was one thing he could say about Beer, it was that he always looked stylish.

Danai looked at himself in the mirror. He did look good, he was wearing skin-tight blue jeans with a pink and yellow polo shirt. His hair was always pretty short, so getting the Thai military haircut the previous year hadn't been a big deal for him. He looked at his face, his skin was perfectly blemish free which he was thankful for, and he started to wonder how Tee saw him. He knew he wasn't as hot as Tee but he felt he was quite good-looking. He was brought out of his vanity by his ringing mobile.

"My boy Da-Nai! What time you at the station man?"

"Nutt's coming by mine at ten, so like ten-thirty or whatever."

"It takes you guys that long to jerk off?"

"You're so funny Noom! Meet us at the station?"

"You know it. Gotta go."

They had a well-practised routine, so they knew exactly where they would meet. On the platform by the advertising pillar just up the stairs to the back of the platform. They'd been doing that for years. They both lived near enough to Chong Nonsi BTS station, so the station was often their meeting point. If they weren't getting on the train they knew to meet outside the 7-Eleven.

THREE

Tee and Fern were the equivalent of a power couple, as far as couples went at Bangkok Silom International School. They had been dating since Grade 7, although both insisted they were just friends. It was curious really, most young people exaggerated and played up their dating exploits. Tee and Fern went to great lengths to play things down. Fern was almost as talented as Tee; she just focused more on academics and so didn't quite add the sporting excellence that Tee did. She was super popular and had a reputation for being one of those genuinely really lovely girls in school. In Grade 10 she had started a programme to help support some of the girls in Grade 6 and 7 who were struggling to fit in at school. Her only fault was her timekeeping, though she was always so apologetic about it that no one ever held it against her, and who was on time for anything in Bangkok anyway?

Danai, Noom and Nutt strutted into MBK trying to look vaguely cool and were surprised to see Tee already there.

"T-bone!" Noom shouted, much to the

embarrassment of his friends. Lots of high-fiving and back-slapping followed as the friends caught up after a few weeks break. Danai suddenly felt slightly flushed and nervous, it annoyed him. He was usually so relaxed with his friends but with Tee he just wanted to say the right thing.

"Hey, Tee."

For fucks sake. Hey Tee. Is that all you can say?

"Danai, nice shirt. I love it. Where did you get that?"

Shit. OMG. He likes my shirt. I think I'm blushing. Be cool.

"Yeah, it's OK. I got it in JJ market."

"Cool, let me know next time you go, you can show me where."

"Nice one."

Nice one. Grrrr. Would that be like a date if I went with Tee to the market?

For the next ten minutes or so as they wandered around the mall, Danai was lost in a daydream. He was amazed how a simple comment from Tee could have such an impact. Tee could move his world with just one word.

"Did you hear about Golf?" Danai finally thought of a conversation topic.

"What's that crazy fuck done now?" Noom fired back.

"Apparently he met the love of his life on holiday in Chiang Mai."

"Awww, that's so cute." Tee smiled so genuinely, it melted Danai again.

"So another one of us gone and got himself a girlfriend!" Noom chipped in.

"Come on guys, me and Fern are just friends." Tee

was bored of reciting this line. "Very good friends."

"Yeah yeah, friends… wiv da benefits!" Noom laughed at his own joke. Danai smiled but it annoyed him so much. He didn't want to think of the love of his life dating Fern. He preferred to remain in the fantasy of his imagination.

"Don't look so sad Danai, we'll get you hooked up soon." Noom put his arm around his best mate and dragged him to look at some clothes, while Nutt and Tee waited by Starbucks for the others.

"That shirt man. It looks seriously good on you. Can't have you looking better than me."

Danai laughed and punched Noom on the arm.

When Fern arrived, giving Tee a big smile and putting her arm around him, it always gave Danai mixed feelings. He liked Fern, he couldn't not really. She was basically a good person. Friendly, funny, and caring. But he hated her too. He hated that she could put her arm around Tee like that. As if she owned him. What gave her the right to do that? He found himself competing with her, subtly, almost unnoticeably, over Tee. Sometimes it would be as simple as walking next to him, or agreeing with Tee. Always agreeing with Tee, especially if Fern had a different opinion.

Sometimes this would annoy Danai inside, even more. She'd laugh and say something like "You boys, always with the same views on clothes." *You boys.* Just like it was a teenage boy thing. She didn't even see Danai as a possible rival for Tee's affections. It was so insulting! But then, he wasn't really a rival for Tee's affection. It was fucking confusing, let's put it that way. Danai was confused himself. He liked her but hated her, or at least wanted to hate her. He was torn by jealousy, he knew that. He wanted to put his arm around Tee, and smile like that at him.

Beem and Golf arrived together, late, and oblivious to how late they were. Once they'd got through the greetings and the gentle mocking of Golf about this apparent girl he'd met, Beem got to the school gossip.

"So, apparently Mr Terry's been sacked. You guys will have a new footie coach this season."

"What the actual? Who told you this? Come on Beem, how the fuck would you know?" Noom interrogated his friend.

"My dad is friends with some of the board members."

"Woah, so what's the story?"

Teachers left, regularly. That was one of the features of an international school. Teachers with the travel bug would move on from country to country. But it was always to a fixed pattern, they'd leave at the end of the year. They'd be an assembly announcement, celebrating those leaving staff. It was always that way. So this was different. Mr Terry was not on that list. He'd talked about football plans for next season, especially with the new Grade 11s as they'd be challenging for the varsity squad.

"Well, my dad wouldn't give the details. But there must be a story there. All very sudden. They got some new bloke from some other Bangkok school." Beem was a bit sketchy.

"Beem. That's total cap. The crummiest gossip ever. There's a story and you don't know what it is, and there's a new coach and you don't know who he is?"

"Yeah, that's pretty much it. But it's true!"

"Interesting, maybe Miss Scott will coach us?" Tee interjected.

"No way Tee. Miss Scott has coached the younger teams forever. She's not gonna suddenly switch now."

"Good point Noom."

The boys continued to muse over the news. They weren't disappointed. Mr Terry had never been that popular, he had something of an old-school style. Shouting and mocking. However, better the devil you know. The boys loved football so much, and it was important to them they had a coach who took it seriously. They were nervous, but also excited at the prospect of a new coach.

FOUR

Despite all the complaining about the impending start of the new school year, there was always an excitement in the air on the first day of term. BSIS had a deserved reputation for being a friendly and laid back school. Students looked forward to seeing most of their teachers again and finding out what the new ones were like. Gossip, usually misinformed, tended to spread fast about new teachers. They also looked forward to seeing their friends, in particular those who weren't quite close enough friends to have seen much over the summer.

It was particularly exciting for Danai and his friends as they were moving into Grade 11. There were special privileges for the seniors in grades 11 and 12. They had some free study periods for example. But the real excitement was reserved for the student lounge. Big comfy chairs, study rooms, hang-out areas, exclusive seniors' café, and even a small kitchen awaited them. The only negative was the big glass window into the office of Miss Waugh, the only dislikeable teacher in an otherwise friendly environment. Miss Waugh was despised, with good reason. The reasons were often even too far-fetched to meet the clichéd stereotype of a nasty teacher. It was practically an open secret in school that she was even more loathed among her colleagues. She particularly hated boys, and if she had any hint they may be gay then she'd hate them even more. Rumour had it that her ex-husband had left her for a man, and that was what took the already bitter and twisted homophobic Miss Waugh over the edge. Every year the school community expected her to be sacked, but every year she remained. The suspicion, and in the eyes of many the only plausible explanation, was that the school was trying to avoid the hassle of firing her. She'd usually be sitting in her office, hunched over, looking much older than her fifty years, with her matted ginger hair often hanging over her face. She walked with a slight stoop that made her look even more witchlike and she had rarely been known to smile.

The Grade 11 students tried to pretend they weren't that interested to know who was in their homeroom groups and who their teachers were, but the truth was that they wanted to know just as much as the younger students.

"Get in! The legend of Danoom survives another year!" Noom gave his best mate a big hug on confirmation that they were still in the same homeroom. Each year they'd discuss how they would approach being split up.

"We fucking strike. I'm serious, man, full-on refusal to go to lessons." Was Noom's suggestion the previous night.

"Who's the homeroom teacher?" Danai asked as his eyes frantically ran down the list for what he really wanted to know. Was Tee in his homeroom?

Tee! Yes! It's all going, Danai! He was thrilled to see Tee's name on the same class list. He wondered if it could be fate. The truth was they wouldn't spend that much time in homeroom groups, but any additional time with Tee was good news as far as Danai was concerned. And it meant he'd be with Tee for PE and those lessons where they talked about sex, drugs, alcohol and everything else.

"Woah! Big Jonesy! It's gonna be a good year."

"I'd prefer to go by Mr Jones, thanks, Noom." The teacher walked by at that precise moment, much to the boy's embarrassment.

"Your dream class Mr Jones, welcome to Danoom!" Noom put out his hand to shake with his teacher. "Dude. Don't leave me hanging, it's humiliating."

Mr Jones looked down quizzically. "Dude? I'll shake your hand when you graduate, Mr Samasuk!" He walked off grinning.

"Burnt! You're such a dick sometimes." Danai was never slow to point this fact out to his best friend.

"What are you so happy about?"

The downside of being part of a double act was that Danai couldn't hide anything from Noom. His friend had immediately noticed how pleased he was on seeing the form lists and he began to wonder what it was that had so pleased him.

Tee arrived soon after, casually walking in but somehow able to wear his school uniform as if he were a fashion model; white shirt perfectly tucked in and not a hair out of place. Danai felt a little rush of excitement through his body, exacerbated by Tee smiling warmly at his friends.

"Good news, T-bone, You're in our class. Danai already noticed." Noom patted Tee's back.

Danai was jolted out of his daydream, but tried to act oblivious.

Why did Noom say that? Does he know? Was he mocking me or just letting me know that he knows?!

"Awesome." Tee smiled and warmly rubbed Danai's shoulder.

"Yeah, it's pretty cool."

Pretty cool? So lame again.

Danai thought to himself that he had to learn to act more normally around Tee.

Miss Scott, one of the most popular PE teachers approached the group. She was well-liked by students and had a reputation for being a bit eccentric and something of an adrenalin junkie. She was always looking for a new extreme sporting activity or competing in triathlons and ultra-marathons.

"Hey, Miss Scott, you absolute nutter!"

"Hi to you too, Noom, how was your summer?"

"Good good. I hear you cycled to China and back! Nutter!"

"Ah. The BSIS rumour mill already in full throttle. I cycled to Chiang Mai, one way."

"Still, that is insane. Legend! Have we got you or Mr Terry for PE this year?" Danai got straight to the point that was already the focus of school gossip.

"Me I think, or could be our new teacher. Not sure."

"Interesting. Very interesting. Why?" Noom asked

with a sarcastic look of high suspicion across his face.

"I don't make the timetables… Danoom!"

"Get in!" The boys high-fived. Miss Scott was one of the few teachers who had also adopted the Danoom tag, and they loved her for it.

"Legend!" Danai screamed as the teacher hurried away to start her day.

"Catch you boys later." This time Tee actually squeezed Danai's shoulder a bit as he spoke. Sending further shivers through the teen's love-sick body.

All the boys were fairly tactile and Noom and Danai were often touching each other in this way. It probably meant nothing. But it was Tee, and so to Danai it meant everything.

FIVE

The first day of term typically began with an assembly, followed by registration in homeroom groups before the drudgery of lessons would actually begin. For most students, assemblies were a pretty dull event. Only the stupidity of the head teacher making some foolish comment would ever ease the boredom.

Rumours about Mr Terry were quickly spreading, and of course, escalating. The most extreme rumour heard was that he was in prison, possibly in Cambodia.

The head teacher strutted onto the stage. Hugh Fowler had a slightly pompous air about him, not helped by his insistence on wearing a gown for school assemblies, not common practice for an international school in Thailand. He spoke in something of a dry and monotone manner which didn't help to pique student interest in what he had to say.

He prattled on. "Welcome back to what we hope will be another fulfilling and successful school year."

"Not for Mr Terry it won't!" Noom whispered.

"You seen Nutt?" Danai asked in an equally hushed tone.

Noom pointed. Classic Nutt. Sitting in the back row on an aisle seat with no one next to him. Obviously he had just slipped in late.

Fowler continued with one cliché after another about challenge and aspiration. The older students waited in hope for one of his famous gaffs.

"I want you all to get a good feel this year, of true success…"

Tee giggled, melting Danai next to him. Even a mature guy like Tee could giggle like a child at times.

The head continued again oblivious "I know for some of you it's hard to get up in the mornings…"

A murmur spread on the back rows of Grade 11 and 12 students.

"Was it hard when you got up?" Noom whispered through a giggle.

On Danai's other side Tee uttered, "I wonder if Fowler can ever get it up!"

Danai fought to supress a full-on laugh.

Mr Fowler did this all the time, clumsy and clueless sexual innuendo. They were relentless and he appeared none the wiser. At the end of the previous school year he had announced a pizza party at lunchtime for the winning house team in school. This resulted in his expressing how much he enjoyed a nine-inch American Hot, but that anything more was too big and much better shared with friends. Most of the staff stood gawping in open-mouthed shock before he continued to explain that this annoyed Mrs Fowler because she preferred a thick Hawaiian.

So by Fowler's standards, today's ones were a bit

tame.

"Finally, I am delighted to announce that our house leaders will stay the same with just one change. Miss Scott will take over from Mr Terry as the head of Ayutthaya House." The four houses in schools were named after the important kingdoms in Thai history: Sukhothai, Ayutthaya, Thonburi and Rattanakosin.

There was a loud cheer for the popular Miss Scott and a general excitement for what appeared confirmation of the fate of Mr Terry. For some students this was essentially verifying the Cambodian prison story.

The sense of first-day excitement continued as students walked to their homerooms for morning registration. Tee and Fern chatted away and Danai wondered if they were upset at being in different groups. There were only three homeroom groups in Grade 11, and of their friendship group Danai, Noom, Tee and Nutt were all in with Mr Jones.

The four of them took the table at the back. Nutt quietly sat down and began sipping on his bottle of Red Bull, the sickly sweet syrupy caffeinated drink.

"Mr Anukunawarakorn, this will be the only time this year I see Red Bull in this room!"

"I'm tired in the morning. Need caffeine."

"Then drink coffee! Add some sophistication, that chemical rubbish is laden with sugar."

"What? I can drink coffee in registration?" Nutt assumed this was a joke.

"Yes, Nutt, you can! This is Grade 11; I don't see why not. No coffee spillages, though."

"Respect, man!"

The boys laughed at this out-of-character comment from the slightly lanky nerd.

"Top bants, Nuttster." Danai patted his back. Nutt smiled, happy with his rare bit of street cred.

"Oh, Jesus, really?" Mr Jones waved his hands to the four boys sat at the back table.

"Come on, Mr Jones, Tee and Nutt can learn to behave themselves." Noom laughed, deliberately misunderstanding what his teacher meant.

Mr Jones smiled knowingly. "Hmm. Good point, Noom. Let's give them a chance."

That sense of first day elation quickly diluted and by the afternoon, students already had that sinking feeling of school being in full swing.

Danai and Noom sat together for the last lesson of the day, history. Mrs Bonner was a no-nonsense teacher. She had a great knowledge of her subject and generally made the topics quite interesting, while treating students with respect. She could be tough but tended to be fair.

"Boys, you can sit together if you want, this is Grade 11 and I am happy to allow you to make your own responsible choices, but maybe think about it?"

Danoom looked at each other before the teacher added "Why don't Danai and Fern swap and then we'll all be happy."

She had barely finished the sentence before Danai jumped up "Yeah that sounds a plan." He tried to hold back his smile. It was like a dream.

Yes! Yes! Mrs Bonner you fucking beauty, I could hug you!

For Danai, this made up for the disappointment of

finding out he was in a different psychology class to all his friends. A complicated twist of the timetable resulting from Danai choosing to study English while all his friends did geography.

Sitting next to Tee might not be good for Danai's growing obsession but it would certainly help his academics. Tee was incredibly conscientious and hard-working. The first day had ended on a high.

SIX

Danai and Noom had arranged to go to the Silom Complex with Beem and Golf to celebrate getting through their first day of school. It was a regular hang-out for at least an hour at the end of the school day, as it was so convenient being right by the Skytrain, which most of them took to go home.

Danai chatted with Tee as they walked to their lockers after the history class. "You coming with us to the mall? There's a few of us going."

"I can't today, I promised I'd walk Fern home."

"Oh, of course, yes. It's getting serious then?"

"Nah, we're just good friends."

Tee carefully placed his books into his locker. In the few hours they'd been at school he had already managed to begin organising his locker with important books to one side, and into neat sections. By the end of the week, Danai knew Tee would also have a colour-coded timetable printed and stuck on the inside of his locker door.

Noom threw things into his locker and would

worry about it later. The result was that he was forever searching for things he'd lost. Danai tended to be somewhere in between the two. He always had great ideas to be neat and organised, but in reality he found it hard to stick to them for a whole term.

"So it's confirmed, Mr Terry is in a Cambodian prison." Noom was typically certain of this now, no discussion. Fact.

"What? How did you find out?" Danai asked.

"You were there, in assembly, Fowler said so."

"He didn't actually say that though…"

"Yeah, he may as well have done."

"Too right he did. Spot on, Noomster, again." Golf and Noom usually shared the same sort of over-exuberance.

The four boys walked off towards the main Silom Road and the mall, as Tee and Fern walked the other way.

"Off to bone her, no doubt!" Golf looked to Noom for approval, they laughed together.

"Tee says they are just friends."

"Danai, don't be so naïve!" Golf shook his head in disbelief.

They walked sensibly to the mall, passing students from St Joseph's Convent School, there was no drama or tension between the different schools. There just wasn't too much of that in this part of Bangkok.

The Silom Complex wasn't the best mall in the city, and the students only went there due to its proximity to school. Generally they'd prefer one of the malls around Siam.

The mall did have plenty of cafés and eateries, otherwise there were lots of beauty-type places and just a few clothes stores that the students liked to browse in. They'd often go to Starbucks to hang out, and then just aimlessly wander the mall before heading home. Beem typically would be playing golf after school so it was something of a rarity for him to join on one of these Starbucks chillouts.

"Starbucks?" Beem asked, but already knew the answer.

"Danai loves Silom Complex Starbucks." Noom winked at his best friend.

"What's that mean?" Danai was genuinely confused.

"Come on, means you can try and flirt with that cute guy who works there."

"Me? I don't know how to flirt." Danai was feeling a bit embarrassed, but technically it was true. His attempts to flirt were abysmal, usually it amounted to him asking a needless question like "Sorry, can I have an extra tissue" and then being super polite.

"Let me count how many times you say, 'thank you' in that cutie voice." Noom laughed and elbowed his best mate.

"You really are a moron sometimes!"

"Enough with your lover's tiff, we need to sort out how I get a date with Nice. She's obviously crazy about me," Golf chirped in.

"Yeah, that's obvious from her rare 'couldn't give a flying fuck' replies to your texts!" This was typical of Beem, he was the quietest of the four but when he chipped in it was usually worth hearing.

The three laughed, much to Golf's irritation.

"This is serious, I'm not fucking about here. She may be the one."

The boys tried to curb their laughter and take their friend seriously. There was always something with

Golf, he was always the most over-the-top. He was the most confident too, and loved himself, even if he probably wouldn't be considered classically good-looking. An unruly mop of hair and a slightly goofy look, nevertheless he was sure he was irresistible to women.

"So, you want to go on a date with her?" Danai was the first to give Golf the serious tone he wanted.

"Duh, yes."

"So…"

"Go on…" Golf was anticipating some words of wisdom.

"Just ask her! Hi, Nice, wanna go to the movies sometime? Job done."

"Oh like you would have the confidence to do that!" Beem politely pointed out.

"Me? No. Golf? Yes, for sure."

"You see, the boy's a genius!" Golf hugged his mate.

"Sorry? What the fuck? Someone tells you if you want to go on a date you ask the girl on a date and this is some sort of genius in your eyes?" Noom screwed his face in mock anger.

"Simplicity, Noomster. This is why you're single, and I am about to be dating the hottest girl any of you haven't met."

The three others looked at each other in confusion and wandered on towards Starbucks while Golf hovered around for a bit to compose his seductive text.

Danai offered to order the drinks as Beem and Noom grabbed a table. The two sat down both glued to their smartphones as Danai went to the counter.

Noom was of course right, his bestie did think one of the workers in Starbucks was very cute. Danai was pleased to see he was on shift and even happier to see he was taking the orders.

"Hi, long time no see!" Danai smiled and blushed, he was impressed that Job recognised him.

"Hey, Job, yes school started today."

"Danai, yes?"

Ooh, he even remembers my name!

They tended to ask names in Starbucks, so they could then call the customers when the drinks were ready. The first time Job had asked Danai his name, he had blushed, thinking that he was chatting him up or something. He guessed Job was about twenty-one or twenty-two and was sure he wouldn't actually be interested in dating a school kid.

"Not too busy today?"

"Nah, it's never really busy at this time." Job winked as Danai walked to the edge of the counter to collect his drinks.

'Not too busy', for fucks sake, that's embarrassing.

He was right, his flirting skills were pretty crap.

The boys chatted away, endlessly flipping from one 'in' joke or conversation topic to another. Someone listening in would have found it hard to follow. So many of the jokes linked back to things that had happened over the years. The advice for Golf was a bit lacking, since none of the boys were actually dating anyone and therefore didn't have much real knowledge about relationships. Though Noom, like Golf, could talk a good game. Beem showed no interest in dating anyone. He was perfectly happy to admit that golf, the sport, was his one true love.

Though of course there were relentless schoolboy jokes about how much Beem loved golf. Beem's doing golf again… or any number of variations on balls and holes. Smutty, childish, but often hilarious.

"So, Terry's a fucking pedo. I swear he used to look at my legs when I played football." Noom brought the conversation back to the school's top gossip.

"Sorry, when did you hear he was a pedo?" Beem asked.

"Cambodia, prison? Come on. It's obvious!"

The other three laughed, this was classic Noom. Two plus two could equal anything, but never four.

"Oh, and incidentally if he was a pedo, he wouldn't be looking at *your* legs." Golf pointed out.

"Exactly! I am glad someone pointed that out," Danai added.

Later that evening Danai lay back on his bed and continued to chat via social media with most of his friends. It was the usual routine. Like most teens in Thailand he preferred to use Instagram most of the time. For group chats, the Line messaging app was the go-to, as you could be more expressive with stickers. There was one huge group that included almost every student in Grade 11, which usually had little of interest. Sometimes there'd be hundreds of crappy messages to trawl through. Invariably this meant you'd miss an important one.

There was a smaller group with his closest friends, which tended to follow a similar pattern to their face-to-face chats.

He most enjoyed his late night texts with Tee. He was much better texting with Tee and trying to flirt over text messaging than in person. They'd often have long and quite deep chats over Instagram messenger but just normal small talk at school or when they'd hang out in a group at weekends. It was the exact opposite to his friendship with Noom. With Noom he obviously wasn't shy face-to-face, but their texting tended to be short, to the point, and usually a whole heap of crap.

He looked through Tee's daily Instagram story, and was pleased to see he had shared a few new pictures. Danai was wearing only a pair of shorts and his hand crept down to slowly rub himself as he looked at his true love. He felt slightly guilty as he did this, like it was too sleazy, too seedy, but he didn't do more than just a gentle rub to get a reaction.

He sent Tee a message and waited. The anticipation was a thrill. How quickly would Tee reply? The disappointment he'd feel if he didn't get a quick reply was immense. It was late, maybe Tee was having an early night. The minutes ticked by, one time his phone buzzed, but his excitement quickly dampened when he saw it was just Noom signing off for the day.

Fuck this shit, gonna sleep. Maybe find some hot videos before I do. 555

555 was uniquely Thai. Five in Thai was 'ha' and therefore the laughing ha-ha-ha could be translated as five five five, hence writing 555 was commonplace for young and old.

After a few minutes, Danai's heart beat just that little faster.

Hey, Danai, good to see you again today.

And you, Tee, always nice to see you ;o) 555

Danai always felt so much more confident expressing himself over text. He never actually told Tee he was attracted to him, he just joked about it a lot, in a way he imagined a gay guy could do with a straight friend.

Ready to try out for the football team?

Danai really wanted to get in the squad, if only to spend more time with Tee, but he wasn't sure if he would get in.

Yeah. Dunno if I'm good enough.

You are. For sure. Speed, good shot, and very fit!

Wow, didn't know you fancied me!

555 you can run for hours. Go to tryouts.

Maybe.

Definitely!

Danai agreed he would, he was touched how keen Tee had been for him to also be in the squad.

He probably says the same to all the guys, or maybe he does love me?

He smiled to himself at his own daydream. They chatted on, Tee talking about his friendship with Fern. He had told Danai before that she was keener on the whole relationship thing. Tee felt school was still too important to get caught up in boyfriend-girlfriend dramas. Eventually Tee said he had to sleep. Their chats usually ended this way, Danai could never bring himself to end a chat, even if he was genuinely exhausted.

SEVEN

As the school year entered its second week, so the students got into their normal school routines. The excitement surrounding the rumours over Mr Terry soon died out as students moved on to other topics. The Grade 11 students were beginning to enjoy the freedom of their student lounge, even if the dreaded Miss Waugh was already proving to be as much of an evil witch as they had heard. She'd frequently push her glasses down her nose to enable her to glare over the top through the big glass window in her office. The students tried to give as good as they got, she was easy to wind up. One particular way was pronouncing her name. She insisted her name was pronounced 'woff' and not the usual 'war'. The kids would try almost anything except the correct one.

Danai was sat doing some maths homework. He had more pressing work but he found maths easier so thought he'd get on with that.

"What the actual fuck, Danai? It's still early in the term why you doing work in here?" Noom pressed his mate.

"Just wanna get it out the way, you know. It's easy."

"You are such a loser! Fucking Waugh's had a go at me today for being like two minutes late."

"She's got nothing better to do." Danai didn't look up from his work.

"Yep, well, I told her I'm in Grade 11, I can be two minutes late."

"Yeah? How did that work out for you?"

With that Noom gently punched his arm. Miss Waugh stood at her door. Her hideous screeching voice bellowed out.

"Errr, Noom! This is a place of study, not chat."

"Sorry, Miss Wag."

"It's Waugh!" she snarled before stomping back into her office.

"What a fucking bitch." Though this time Noom whispered.

"We going to the mall today, D-boy?"

"We won't feel like it after football trials."

"Yeah, true. Trials will be easy, we'll both coast into that squad!" Noom slouched off to the small kitchen to make himself a snack. He was supremely confident about making it, probably over-confident, but they certainly both had a decent shout.

Tee had a free lesson, so he headed off to the sports centre to find Miss Scott. She would supervise the football trials as the new coach had only been in the school for two weeks. Tee had been appointed the new captain by Mr Terry at the end of the previous school year. No one was surprised, he was the best player in school but also very popular with all the other players.

He knocked on the open door. "Miss Scott, can I have a quick word?"

"Of course, Tee, how you doing?" Miss Scott looked up to give Tee her full attention.

"Very good. Looking forward to trials today."

"Should be a good team this year I reckon."

"Yes for sure. Have you got a good idea who will be picked?" he politely asked, with a look on his face that made it clear he was trying to move to his key point.

"I hope you are not suggesting that's it's all pre-determined!"

"No no, I don't mean that, just asking."

"Relax, Tee, I'm kidding. It should be competitive, sadly some will miss out." She sat back in her chair. Miranda Scott always had a welcoming openness that students appreciated. It was sub-conscious but she wanted to make sure Tee was relaxed and could say what he needed to get off his chest.

"Do you think Danai has a chance, Miss?"

"Danai? Yes for sure, he did well last year. Tougher in the senior squad though."

"I think he'd be good. He's fast, and he can score goals. Be a good winger."

"You may be right. Is this when you hand me a bribe?"

This time Tee laughed. "Would you take a bribe miss?"

"If it was enough for me to retire and buy a mansion in Phuket, we can talk."

"Well, I got like a hundred baht on me." Tee smiled.

"I will have a good look at Danai today, for sure."

"It'd be cool, he's got a good attitude. If I had a captain's pick…"

"Then it would become a mad house! Leave it with me Tee, and thanks for the chat." She smiled back and he thought she might have given him a subtle wink.

"Oh, and please don't tell Danai I spoke to you; he'd probably be mad at me."

"No problem, skipper. But if Danai is picked, he is picked on merit because he's good enough."

Miss Scott was amazed by Tee's maturity; he had obviously noticed that Danai could do with the confidence boost. She would never tell Tee that she picked Danai on his advice. He was always going to be in with a great chance of making the squad, but Tee's intervention had secured his spot.

There was always an excitement on the day of football trials, which was followed by tears, elation and debates about the merits of the squads the coaches had picked. By Grade 11 it was even tougher, they were competing with the Grade 12 students and only fifteen would make the elite squad. There were around twenty-six who turned up for the trials. There were always four or five who were never going to make it but the rest of the decisions would be tough. Golf, Beem, and Nutt dragged their bags to the pitch, having decided to watch and support their friends.

"Shoot!" Beem randomly screamed as he walked to the pitch, the boys were warming up.

Miranda Scott took the selection process very seriously because she knew how much it meant to the boys, which she explained to the new coach John

Jameson. He clearly had a similar attitude; football was his main sport and he arrived at BSIS from one of the other international schools in the city.

"You'll find Tee not just a good captain, but a really mature kid," she whispered to John on the touchline.

"Yep, I've already got that vibe from just one PE lesson so far. So polite."

"Yeah. He's sickeningly perfect! Wait until you see him play." She smiled and gathered the students around and quickly explained the process. It sounded slightly chaotic, they'd basically play a 7-a-side and she'd keep swapping players in and out. Miranda explained the system to the boys and added her usual British joke that football was football and soccer was not a word to be uttered in the presence of British PE teachers. The boys groaned and laughed; they'd heard it many times.

Tee had a quick word with Danai before they started playing. "Use that pace of yours down the wings Danai, that'll be sure to get you noticed."

"Thanks, Tee, feed me some good passes then!"

"Always." He winked and walked off to take the kick-off.

The games were intense but played in a good spirit. The coaches changed the players frequently, and each time the boys try to second-guess what it meant. The optimists told themselves Miss Scott could see they were good enough and had pencilled them in, others felt they were being taken off as they were not up to standard.

Tee spent long periods watching the games near enough to Miss Scott and Mr Jameson for them to hear his shouts of encouragement or his blatant attempts to praise his closest friends. Noom played very well, he was a dependable defender and was always going to be in the squad. For all his goofiness he became very serious once he got on the pitch. Danai's best moment came late in the game. Tee picked him out with a perfectly weighted pass, Danai beat the defenders and crossed for his captain. Tee unselfishly played a simple pass back to his friend who smashed the ball into the far corner. If that made him feel elated, what followed was like a dream; Tee ran towards him hugged him and lifted him in the air. Later on Danai would think about how quickly it happened, and how he wished he had savoured it more. He could feel Tee's muscular arms, he rubbed and patted Tee's back and breathed in his sweat. If he didn't make the squad, he'd always have this moment.

"Yo the man!" Noom screamed from the touchline. Nutt leapt in the air.

"Since when did you care about the school football team?" Noom asked his usually quiet, calm and slightly nerdy mate.

"Gotta support the boys Noom. Danai's been fucking awesome."

"Yeah, I gave him a pep talk before the game."

Noom observed carefully, wondering just why Nutt was so animated.

Miss Scott did a quick end-of-game chat with the boys, reiterating how tough it would be and properly introducing Mr Jameson who would be the official coach of the senior team.

"I know I can speak for Mr Jameson too when I say how impressed we have been. The standard is amazingly high this year. The list will be up tomorrow morning and Mr Jameson will start the training sessions from next week."

The only thing the boys really listened to was when the list would go up. They trudged off to collect their bags and head home.

"Danai! Wait up!" Tee shouted across the school car park.

Fuck, he can even have the energy to run after all that football.

"You were awesome today. You gotta make the squad." Tee gave a huge smile, with his perfect teeth just adding to his beauty in Danai's eyes.

"Thanks, and thanks for that pass. That goal might help!"

"Wanna pop to the mall for a cold drink?" Tee casually asked.

"Yeah, cold drink that's good, yeah why not, I mean I have time."

What the fuck! Just say yes. Fuck, he loves me. It's a date!

"Cool, can't stay too long, my mum will hassle me about homework."

"Yeah, same."

Better. Keep it simple.

They walked towards the Silom Complex, chatting as they went, and Danai began to feel a bit more relaxed.

"So how's things with Fern?" As they sat down in Starbucks, Danai decided to be bold.

"Fern's awesome, she's my best friend, you know?"

"Yeah, you guys are always together."

"We've been friends since Grade 6. She's cool."

"Just friends? Really?" Danai try to sound cool, but he was so curious.

"Yes. I know no one believes me but I just don't want a girlfriend at school. Work, sport, university places. Got to focus."

"What does Fern want though?"

"Hey, you're like some counsellor genius. That's the thing, she wants us to be more serious." Tee sighed.

"Go with the flow T-bone." As he said it Danai almost winced. Go with the flow. T-bone, he'd heard that bullshit from Noom. What the fuck.

Tee laughed, revealing the most beautiful smile Danai had ever seen. "You been spending too much time with Noom! T-bone?"

They took a selfie, on Tee's insistence as a memory of the day they played in the football trials. "Start of a new era in BSIS football."

Danai looked at the photo as he went to bed. He day dreamed that one day they'd be happily married and this photo would be framed in their tasteful home.

His phone buzzed; he grabbed it hoping it was a goodnight message from Tee. Predictably it was Noom.

Good football today, D-boy. You be in.

Thanks, man, you'll make it too.

Did you know Nutt liked football? Noom asked.

Nutt's a man of mystery!

Yeah, think he might fancy you. Noom casually responded.

WHAT? WTF? What the actual fuck? Danai was genuinely shocked to hear this.

Whatevs. Chat tomorrow.

He wasn't sure what to make of the comments about Nutt, but he eventually fell asleep with thoughts of him, Tee, and their two adopted kids. Living happily ever after.

EIGHT

Danai woke just before his alarm went at six-thirty am. He usually only needed thirty minutes at home to shower, grab some breakfast, and give him enough time to get to school before seven-thirty. He was particularly excited knowing that Miss Scott would have put the team list up as soon as she got in. He wanted to get in early, fearing looking at the list with all his mates around and having to deal with a crushing blow. Although he tried to keep a bit of healthy pessimism, he felt quite confident. He had played well, Tee had rightly noticed that and this year the Grade 12 students were not that strong, there was likely to be more than half from Grade 11.

He managed to get into the shower before his older brother, Beer. This wasn't usually a challenge as Beer rarely woke up early, but for some reason today he had decided to go into university early, something about meeting friends for coffee to discuss a group project. He banged on the door.

"Don't be too long, Danai, no jerking off!"

"Fuck off!" Danai shouted back.

How does he know I usually jerk off in the shower? He laughed at himself for even pondering this, as the reason why all boys knew that boys jerked in the shower was pretty obvious.

He wasn't planning on it anyway; he was in a hurry this morning. Though if he closed his eyes he could try and imagine the feel and smell of Tee when they hugged on the pitch. He stopped himself from daydreaming, wrapped a towel around himself and stood looking in the mirror. He was in pretty good shape, even if he didn't have the sculptured torso of his school crush.

He walked to his room and began to get his clothes ready. Beer appeared at the door. "Good luck today little bro, you'll make it. I'm sure."

"Thanks, Beer."

It was quite sweet of his older brother really. He sometimes feigned a lack of interest in his younger brother's life, but when it came down to it he did know what was going on, and he did care.

His parents were both sitting in the kitchen when he walked downstairs. They were very early risers; his mum often went for a run before six and his dad tended to meditate first thing.

"Want some rice and pork sweetie?" his mum asked.

"No time, got to get to school early."

Usually one of them would tell him he should have a good breakfast. Neither did, they both knew why he was going in early and how important it was to him.

"Remember, what will be will be. You'll do great this year whatever happens today." His dad's words were a bit clumsy but he knew what he meant.

"Is Noom coming for dinner tonight?" Danai's mum was always happy for Noom to come over.

"Maybe. Bye. See you!" He dashed out the house a bundle of nervous energy.

He arrived at school about twenty minutes earlier than usual, it was eerily quiet. He had hit that spot just before the mad rush of students arriving. Perfect. He walked towards the sports centre and up the stairs to the main noticeboard.

"I've been waiting ages!" Tee was sitting down on the floor by the main board. Danai was surprised to see him there, and scratched his head while look down. He did also feel a flutter of excitement at the realisation that Tee was waiting there for him.

"Have you looked?" Danai stuttered as he softly spoke.

"No, was waiting for you." Tee grinned in the way that only Tee could.

"But you didn't know I was coming in early…" Danai tailed off quietly.

"Oh, I knew. Noom will be here in ten minutes, not *too* early or he'll worry that we'll think he's nervous!"

They both laughed.

He walked towards the noticeboard and started nervously looking for his name. It jumped right out at him. DANAI. Miss Scott had written all the names in capitals. There he was, just beneath TEE.

"Yes! Get in! I mean I always knew." He laughed.

Tee gave him a warm pat on the back and winked as he said, "I made it too!"

He continued to stare at his name. *Just underneath Tee too, like one of my dreams.* He laughed as he thought this with Tee standing a foot away.

"I'm so happy for you, Danai, we are gonna be an awesome team this year."

"Yo! My two teammates, how you doing?" Noom swaggered down the corridor, earlier than Tee predicted.

"Who said you were in?" Danai spoke in a deadpan manner.

"Come on. Wait, what. Am I?" Noom's swagger had gone.

Tee walked towards him "I'm really sorry, dude, maybe next year."

They couldn't keep the joke going, seeing the look of horror on Noom's face. The two boys began laughing.

"You fucking idiots, I didn't believe you anyway, let me just see…" He looked to the board. "There it is. N-O-O-M, yes, Miss Scott knows a top versatile player when she sees one!" It was true, Noom was perhaps the one player who could play in any position; midfield, defence, and in attack. He had done it all in the under-sixteen team.

The three friends chatted excitedly about the upcoming season, how great it was that all three were in the squad and how they were going to lead BSIS to glory. Bangkok Silom International School had a decent reputation for their football team, but they had always been the nearly boys of Bangkok school football. Twice they had been losing finalists in the Bangkok Schools' Cup as well as being runners-up in the Bangkok School League on as many occasions. The Grade 11 trio were determined to put it right.

Danai texted his brother and parents who were all happy for him, before he headed to morning registration. Lessons that day were pretty uneventful, and boring, but Danai didn't care. All he could think about was how happy he was to have made the team and the added joy of all the extra time he would get to spend with Tee. In his naughtier moments he considered the opportunities he might get to see Tee's body. He felt guilty thinking like this though, football was important to him and so he didn't want to stereotype himself as only really being interested in a sexy smooth cute guy. He was usually brought out of these daydreams by a teacher asking him a question or a friend grabbing his attention.

That evening, he sat on his bed while Noom lounged on the small armchair in his bedroom.

"I'm really happy for you to have made that team you know?" Noom moved to sentimental and serious mode.

"Ah. So sweet, I didn't know you cared so much." Danai instantly felt he was being too sarcastic, Noom genuinely looked out for him.

"And as a bonus you get to spend so much time with all the fittest boys in school." He laughed and threw a small cushion at his friend.

"Shut up. Who told you I was into boys?" It was a soft almost casual protest.

"Oh, Danai! No one has to tell me; you've been my closest friend since forever."

They both laughed and Danai hurled the cushion back at Danai, missing and knocking some books off the shelf.

"And *that* is why you're in the soccer team and not the basketball team! Anyway, there must be someone in the team you have your eye on?"

"Nah. Whatever. Just wanna play well. What about you? Who's your eye on?"

"Anyone! I'm so horny these days, never even kissed a girl. This is the year. Maybe for you too?"

"Maybe." He giggled, thinking about Tee.

"Aha! You see, there is someone. You were thinking about him just now! Admit it?!"

"I admit nothing, Noom! Never!" They laughed, and then an awkward silence hung in the air.

Noom suddenly reacted excitedly. "Oh shit, I forgot…Nutt!"

"Oh yeah what was that bullshit you texted last night?"

"It's not BS, man, you know I can tell this stuff. He came there to watch you. He was desperate for you to do well."

"Come on, Nutt? Nutt's never fancied anyone or anything. Well, maybe a maths equation?" Danai dismissed the idea, it just seemed plainly absurd.

Noom spoke. "Anyway, he'd be lucky to have you, just like, whoever it is you're in to…You're boyfriend material, and so hot too!"

"So not just me into guys then?" Danai's laugh was a bit forced. Noom was straight, as far as he had ever known.

"Not really, D-boy, but you know me man. I don't do labels. I'm Noom. I'm just me. Uniquely Noom."

"I can't work out if that's pretentious or just stupid!"

"I'm serious Danai. I'm not into you, but I can still

see you're cute! I'd kiss you buddy."

"This is too weird, you're my best mate."

"Yeah we wouldn't kiss like that, I mean we'd kiss to know what it's like."

The tension was broken by Noom's mum shouting them downstairs for dinner.

"Saved by my mum!" Danai winked. Noom walked over and kissed his friend on the forehead. "Next time I mean a real, sloppy, wet kiss!"

NINE

Beem was in his room practising his golf swing, and then grabbed his putter and a ball to play a few short putts on his indoor practice putting mat. He had a big tournament at the weekend, and now that he was sixteen, the competition was getting harder. He was under no illusions about how difficult it would be to make it as a pro, but it will still his dream. It seemed to be fate when he became best friends with Golf at school, he'd often wondered if Golf's name had been something different, would they have become best friends?

His phone buzzed. It was Golf.

What you doing?

Nothing man. You?

He didn't need to tell his mate he was practising his putting rhythm.

Just near your home, let me in. There in 2.

It was classic Golf. He rarely checked to see if it was a good time, he just texted when he was close to the house.

They had become good friends when they joined BSIS, even though their personalities were so different. In their own way they were both outsiders, to a degree. Beem hailed from the Isan region in Thailand's North East. He was darker skinned than most of his friends who were of Thai-Chinese descent. His friends often joked with him about it. People from Isan tended to be stereotyped as being less educated and doing all the low-paid menial jobs in the country.

For Golf, it was that his dad was German, although it wasn't easy to tell, he certainly looked more Thai than German. He often joked that his Thai genes must have been stronger. But there were instances when he felt different from the Thai crowd, and some awkward times when people joked about foreigners marrying Thai women who they'd met in some of the dodgier bars in Bangkok.

Golf was polite and friendly with Beem's parents when they let him in, and then he traipsed up to his friend's room.

"So, the boys all made it into the football squad," Golf spoke in a serious tone.

"Shit yeah, did they? I forgot to ask." Beem had completely forgotten during the day at school.

"Yeah, all three, it's awesome."

"That's why they were so happy today!" Beem had wondered what the excited mood was but never thought to ask.

"Classic. Why didn't you ask? Too busy thinking about balls and holes." Golf chuckled.

"You'll never get tired of that joke, will you?"

"You know it!"

Beem could sense Golf wanted to speak about something, he wasn't his usual relaxed self. Typically Golf would just start talking a thousand words a minute, putting on music, and showing his friend some funny memes he'd seen that day. After a while, he spoke, "You think I should ask Nice out?"

"Sure. You said you liked her. Go for it." It seemed pretty obvious to Beem.

"Yeah, I guess." Golf quietly clicked his tongue and moved his mouth around, wondering what to say.

"So…" Beem sounded a bit more irritable than he had planned.

"I don't know how to go about it. What should I do?"

Beem smiled, a confused grin. "You're asking me? How the fuck would I know?"

"You never wanted to ask someone out?" The goofy grin had gone as Golf continued in his serious mode.

"Nope. Never. No interest. Is that weird?" His head tilted slightly to the left.

"No man, it's not weird. You're busy with golf. No time for dating!"

"Exactly. So why you acting like it's such a dilemma?"

"I don't know." He said with the lack of conviction of someone who clearly did know.

"Well, what about the girl you dated last year? Or

what's her name when we were in Grade 8, how did you ask her out?"

"Err…." Golf clenched his teeth, nervously.

"Err, what? What you mean?"

"For fuck's sake, Beem, I never actually dated Ploy, or Pim." He gazed down as if studying something on the floor.

"What the fuck? What do you mean? You spoke about it all the time, when you kissed and all that."

Golf's head remained lowered, gingerly. He said nothing.

Beem felt awkward, he was uncomfortable with this sort of heart-to-heart conversation but knew his best mate needed him. "Don't worry about it man. Let's work out what you can text her." Golf didn't respond. "Just be simple, like ask her if she wants to hang out next weekend. You know. What they do in movies!"

"I feel like such a loser." Golf sounded genuinely downbeat.

"Golf! You're the most confident person I know. Don't talk like that!"

"It's fake, Beem, I thought you knew this. I play this act all the time, man. I'm sick of it. Nice won't want to date me."

"Right, you're not leaving here until you've texted her. I'll ring Tee!"

"He'll laugh at me." Golf knew that wasn't true. Tee would never laugh at anyone. It was a standing joke, but a truism as well, that Tee was the nicest guy that any of them knew. He was more mature than them all too, so was constantly being called for advice and support.

Beem video called him on Instagram. When Tee

answered he was walking outside, he looked a bit moody or upset.

"Hey, Beem. What's up, dude?"

"Just here with Golf, you OK?"

"Yeah, man, I'm cool, just walking fast and sweating, going home from Fern's."

"You dirty boy, Tee!" Golf shouted.

Tee smiled but sighed at the same time. "Golf's there too I take it?" He got bored of trying to convince people that he wasn't having sex with Fern, so he just ignored it.

They didn't get deeply into Golf's issues, but just casually asked Tee what he'd advise. He didn't say anything mind-blowing, but his theme of be yourself, chill out, don't worry about it, did help to relax Golf. After the call ended he messaged Nice, and waited for a reply.

Beem chatted about school and random shit to stop Golf nervously checking the phone. Then he suddenly remembered something.

"Hang on, when you told me in great detail about kissing Ploy and how she jerked you off…"

"Leave it, Beem!"

His phone buzzed. "Well well, she does love a bit of Golf after all!"

"She said yes?"

"She fucking did, man, this time I might be really getting jerked off." He sort of screamed and laughed at the same time.

Beem smiled. He was pleased to see Golf back into his usual mood. It was amazing to see how quickly he could switch back to the default happy Golf they all loved.

TEN

By early October the school year was already in full swing, the excitement of entering Grade 11 had long since worn off. The added pressures of more specialised study were becoming stressful. Even the novelty of having a study area, the little kitchen, and some chill out spaces had become less of a focal point. The football season was soon to be starting with some real matches, and for the players in the squad this was their main motivation for school.

Danai, Tee, and Noom spent most of their spare time discussing the upcoming matches, who their big challengers were and if they had a chance to win the prestigious Bangkok Schools' Championship. They had begun to warm to the new coach, Mr Jameson, after the usual initial trepidation of a new teacher who had at first seemed very serious. He *was* indeed serious when it came to football and training but once they had got into a good training routine the boys found he could engage in some good banter. He was every bit as popular as Miss Scott with the kids, well mainly the sporty kids. He didn't find it as easy to engage with students who didn't enjoy sport. They trained every Monday and Thursday after school and he was more than happy to add additional training sessions, as the boys liked.

The opening match was at home, on a Wednesday after school — the traditional day for the Under-18 senior team matches. They were due to play one of the better teams, St Christopher's Academy, a purely British International school with a very high academic standard, but also annoyingly good at sport.

The Monday training was a light session to ensure they would all remain sharp for the game on Wednesday. There was a nervousness in the squad as they all wondered who would be in the starting seven for the game. They'd be five substitutes, so three of the squad of fifteen were certain to miss out. It was only the first game but it usually set down a marker for the season.

"One minute, collect all the balls, grab a drink and gather by the side," Mr Jameson barked his orders at the end of the session. The boys all sat down as he went into a general patter about the game and tactics. Tee winked at Danai and clenched his fist in encouragement. "Right, twelve of you will be involved on Wednesday. It will be intense; you'll all be getting good game time. The three who miss out, your time will come…" They were the usual encouraging words they were used to hearing. The first part was true of course, in the heat of Bangkok and the energy of school football the substitutes would be important. They all wanted the pride of starting the game though.

"Tee, of course."

Tee did an expression of mock surprise, the boys laughed which broke the tension.

"Big Sam in nets, Tee and Noom in defence, Jam and Den either side of Not in midfield, and Nik up front."

Danai tried not to look disappointed, but Noom and Tee knew how he'd feel. He almost missed the last words of Mr Jameson as he went through the substitutes "….and last but definitely not least, Danai. We'll need that pace of yours."

There was lots of cheers and hugs and awkward commiserating of the players who had missed out.

"The three amigos are in!" Tee cheerfully announced.

"Amigos? Aren't we the musketeers?" Noom laughed.

"Well you two are in, I'm only a sub." Danai knew he should have been happy but couldn't help but feel he was missing out.

"Shut the fuck up, Danai! You heard him. He deliberately put you on the bench because of your pace." Noom was adamant, and Tee backed him up. It was a classic tactic, keep the fastest player back a bit for when the opposition were tired. It might have been a strategy from Tee to cheer him up, if so, it worked. Danai had a bit more of a spring in his step as Tee put his arm around him as they walked out of school.

It always felt so good when Tee was tactile with him in this way, just feeling his arm around him was a thrill. It was usually followed by guilt, at having this secret crush. Did it make him one of those creepy stalker types?

I'm telling Tee how I feel. Just not this year. When it's the right time. When we've left school. When he's broken up with Fern.

These sort of things often went around Danai's head.

He walked home alone from the Skytrain station, Noom and Tee going off together in the other direction. He sometimes wished he lived where Noom did, on the same road as Tee. He got in and went for a shower. He thought about those communal showers that you see in movies. If school had those, he could see Tee's body, every part of Tee's body. He felt himself getting hard as he washed himself carefully and decided to jerk off. It didn't take long, he closed his eyes and visualised Tee in his football kit, sweat glistening off his muscular arms. He often wondered how Tee would look naked, he was sure he would look even more amazing. Everything about Tee was better than everyone else, so it followed that his dick would be better too. After he had finished and then cleaned up he laughed at the idea of what exactly a 'better dick' was. He had no idea.

The boys thought about the match with St Christopher's, and little else, during school on Tuesday and Wednesday. They gathered in the changing rooms before the match to get out of their school uniform and into their football kit. Danai was always fascinated by how fastidious Tee was with his clothes. Many would just stuff their clothes into their bag or locker, Tee would carefully fold everything and leave it neatly. Perhaps he worked in a clothes shop in a previous life.

Danai didn't miss the opportunity to glimpse at Tee's body. He wouldn't be naked but he'd get down to his tight-fitting boxer-briefs, which was a thrill enough. Danai would quickly switch his school trousers for his shorts, but he noticed Tee was much more comfortable just wearing his boxers. Probably because his body was such perfection. There was a nice bulge too, Danai could only imagine what was underneath the skin-hugging material.

As was always the case for home matches, a big crowd would gather from all year groups in school. Some of the younger students were in awe and dreamed of a future where they were playing in front of a crowd like this. Golf was in charge of a small cheering squad with Beem, Fern, and Nutt. He joked that they were the wives and girlfriends cheering squad.

"Sorry? Who am I supposed to be married to?" Nutt enquired.

"Take your pick, Nutty!" They all laughed.

Fern was the only one who felt she was genuinely dating one of the team, even if her boyfriend didn't see it quite the same way.

"Go, Silom!" Golf roared as the players arrived to warm up. He patted Danai's shoulder and implored him to 'give 'em hell', which seemed better than the banal 'score a goal or whatever', that Beem added.

"How does Tee's hair even look perfect when he plays football?" Beem commented, matter of fact.

Fern smiled.
"He does spend some time perfecting it."
Even while he was playing Noom would glance towards Nutt, determined to see if his theory was correct and if he was checking out Danai. It was obvious, even to those who weren't big football fans, that it was going to be a hard game. The St Christopher's team were physically strong and dominated the early stages, scoring a goal after about ten minutes. Not looked devastated but the consensus from the side was that it wasn't his fault. The opponent's striker was one of the best players in the league and had even been called up to the Thai youth squad.

"Think they're gonna win?" Nutt asked Fern.

"Hope so, but it looks tough. Didn't know you like football?"

"I can't stand the game, but just want to support my friends."

Fern giggled. "I'm starting to like soccer a bit more, I have to watch so many matches dating Tee."

"How can he be so fucking good at everything?" Nutt was genuinely stunned at how this was possible.

"I know, I know. Even worse he doesn't really realise it." Fern giggled.

"So fit too!" Nutt winked at Fern who blushed a little.

Golf and Beem were much more intently watching the game. "Jameson's a fucking nutter. Who knew?" Golf observed. The coach was certainly passionate, barking orders and encouragement constantly. Mid-way through the first half he signalled for Danai to get ready. His mini fan club cheered;

Golf also noticed a big grin from Nutt.

"This is it, Danai baby!" Noom screamed from his defensive position alongside Tee. Danai was deep in discussion with his coach, oblivious. His impact was instant, running at pace, dragging players around and forcing an error from the defence which resulted in Tee blasting home from just outside the penalty area for the team's first goal of the season. The celebrations were wild on and off the pitch, hugs all round.

The players trotted off for half-term and a stirring team talk from their coach.

"Danai, you little fucking beauty!" Mr Jameson wouldn't normally swear at school, but the passion and excitement of football was a different story. "We've got this, boys, you hung in there well and we're on top now. Keep strong. Tee keep working, track back. Noom and Not, love it. Strong and tough, just don't slide in and over commit."

As they walked back onto the pitch for the 2nd half Tee slapped Danai on the ass, "Same again D." He held his hand there for a split second. Danai had to concentrate not to have the embarrassment of getting a hard-on, right there on the pitch.

"Did you see Waugh's face there? She heard Jameson swearing. Didn't look impressed." Golf observed.

"Fucking bitch." It was a rare outburst from Nutt, but Miss Waugh was uniquely unpopular around the school.

"Danai's playing well isn't he?" It was time for Golf to fish a little bit.

"Yep, awesome, he's made a big difference I

think." Golf was sure Nutt's eyes glazed over a bit as he spoke.

The second half was just as tough, with Jameson using the roll-on, roll-off substitutions to his full advantage as the boys tired. Noom was given nearly ten minutes rest in the second half, only Tee played for the full hour. The end was one of pure joy as Nik scrambled in a winner with almost the last kick of the game. It was only the start of the season but the boys celebrated like they had won the trophy. To beat one of their big rivals in such a tough and competitive fixture meant something. Mr Jameson gave a quick congratulatory chat, full with the usual platitudes that it was only one game and there was a long way to go.

Danai was exhausted and deliriously happy, as he lay on his bed late that night. Everything seemed to be going his way at the moment. Life was good. His phone buzzed. It was Tee.

Awesome today buddy, thanks to you we got back in the game.

Aww. Thanks, Tee. I enjoyed it. Nice goal too.

Tee replied with a smile. It was a brief exchange as they were both tired. But it meant so much to Danai. It was usually always him who started a chat. So for Tee to do so, was a thrill. He giggled with excitement.

He's thinking about me. He's at home, about to go to bed, and he's thinking about me. Me!

ELEVEN

On Thursday morning Danai was chatting with Noom, Golf, and some others in the common room when Mr Jameson walked in. He went over to the boys, focusing on his footballers.

"How are the muscles feeling today boys?"

Golf laughed. "They've been moaning all morning!"

Mr Jameson wasn't surprised. "Always the way with the first game of the season, boys. That was a proper hard work out."

Miss Waugh appeared from her office, skulking, pinched face. She spoke in her trademark shrill squeak. "Mr Jameson, can I have a quick word?"

It was the same tone that she'd use to summon students for a 'chat'.

"Of course, Miss Waugh." He pronounced her name wrong, by accident, but some of the boys laughed, much to her irritation.

Noom crept over to the door so he could listen in.

"I have to say I don't think it's very professional

that you were swearing during the match yesterday." She spoke like she was disciplining him.

He wasn't sure whether to take it seriously, at first he grinned. "Yeah, the passions of sport runs that way at times."

"Well, I don't think it's acceptable."

Noom imagined her face contorted in that typical way.

"Oh, I see, well, I wouldn't normally of course, but it's true that sports fixtures tend to be a bit different from a normal classroom setting…" He was still not quite sure if this was some sort of joke.

"I don't want to hear it again, or I will be making a formal complaint." She raised her voice, increasing in irritation that the football coach wasn't taking her seriously.

"Sorry, you are actually serious!" He laughed and shrugged, as if to say, 'Do as you must.'

"And another thing, this is a study room, you shouldn't be here without a good reason."

There was a brief period of silence, Noom wished he could see the expression on either of the teacher's faces.

He slowly walked away from the door as he heard Mr Jameson. "Well, it's been pleasant chatting, you have yourself a lovely day." He walked out and clearly gave Noom a knowing wink, as Noom rushed over to tell his friends exactly what he had heard.

Danai immediately sent Tee a Line message and within minutes the whole football squad knew what had happened. John Jameson had already been gradually winning the respect of the boys, and this sealed his legendary status. He wasn't going to put up with any bullshit from Allison Waugh.

Tee sat down at lunch, opposite Fern, as usual. He tended to have lunch with Fern and her friends. If he didn't, she'd get annoyed. He wasn't far from the boys, who usually sat at the opposite end of the long table. On the occasions he did sit with them he quickly realised it was a lot more fun. Fern had been pretty much his best friend ever since they'd been in primary school. They had enjoyed being paired together in class when they were in Grade 6 and both had a fastidiousness that suited the other. As they became teenagers their friendship still remained strong but the pressures from Fern to take their relationship to the next level, and beyond, stressed him out. It wasn't something he wanted. It wasn't that he didn't find her attractive, she was obviously very good-looking, it was just it wasn't a big deal for him. All his male friends seem to be permanently horny and talking about when they'd have sex. If they'd had sex. Who they would like to have sex with. He just didn't have the same feelings.

Fern assumed that he would come round eventually, surely by the time he was eighteen and at university they'd have something physical. They had kissed, but he never wanted to use his tongue and she could tell it wasn't something he was passionate about. It was the exact opposite of the movie stereotype where it was a teen boy trying to persuade his girlfriend to take things further.

"Did you hear about Mr Jameson today?" he asked Fern.

"No." She seemed a bit disinterested and carried on another conversation with her girlfriends.

"Always about sport and sport teachers with these

boys!" Ploy laughed.

Fern gave Tee a bit of a glare. "Why don't you just go and sit with the boys and talk about football then!" She joined in with the girls laughing, Tee happily took the bait and moved down the table to sit with the lads.

"Trouble in paradise, T-bone?" Golf teased.

"Yeah, you know how it is." Tee winked back.

"So what's he gonna do about that fucking bitch?" Golf continued the conversation at the table. Tee immediately knew that they were discussing the Waugh-Jameson confrontation.

"We'll have to invite Jameson to sit with us at lunch and bitch about her."

"Wow, Tee! I've never seen you get so angry." Beem spoke, but it could have been any of them, they'd all noticed the anger in the football captain's voice.

"What you boys up to this weekend?" Danai couldn't help but look at Tee when he asked, as that's what he really wanted to know.

"Well, your mum keeps asking me for dinner, maybe I'll come to yours on Friday night." It was a common event that Noom stayed over at Danai's on a Friday evening.

"Danai, no offence buddy but I'm sure your mum fancies Noom." Golf laughed as he spoke, it was something he had repeated regularly over the years.

"You are sick!" Danai kicked him under the table.

"Hey, come on. Nothing wrong with me recognising that your mum's an attractive woman."

"Yeah, it's a fair comment, D, she does like a bit of Noom, must be my smile." He grinned as he got in on the mocking.

"Is it always like this down this end of the table?" Tee asked Danai. Tee was sat close to Danai and his leg was very gently touching his friend's. Danai felt a thrill run through his body, he wanted to let out a soft moan.

"Yeah, we just try to ignore Golf and Noom when they're like this."

"Just cos us two appreciate the older woman." Golf high-fived Noom.

Danai shook his head. As it happened it was partly true, Noom was definitely his mum's favourite among his friends. But that's where it ended. The rest was just stuff of ridiculous teenage fantasies. Luckily Golf changed the subject by telling them all about his weekend plans with Nice. They were going to hang out around the Siam area and maybe see a movie.

After lunch Danai had English followed by Psychology. All his friends had Psychology and then Geography. They had quickly worked out that on a Thursday Mr Stevens just delivered the identical Psych lesson to both classes, back to back.

"It's mad some of this psychology shit, but during the last lesson of the day, I sometimes zone out sitting in the back glaring out the window."

"Oh, you sit at that window seat in the corner too?" Tee asked.

"Yep, best seat in class, I glare out at the football pitch." Danai smiled back.

"Ha-ha. Same. I'll leave you a note next time." Tee winked and sent another shiver right through his friend's body.

Danai could think about little else during his English lesson, he daydreamed that Tee would confess his love in a note left on his seat in the lesson. How romantic. He would never admit it to anyone, he even privately felt embarrassed about it but when he knew he had a lesson in the same classroom directly after Tee, he'd rush as fast as he could just to get a glimpse before he'd left the classroom. Just to say hi. Just to see his sweet smile. This must be how love feels.

His English teacher kept them a bit late, setting some homework and additional research, which was frustrating. When he arrived down on the first floor for psychology, he was too late. The room was empty, apart from Mr Stevens.

"Afternoon, Danai. Good win yesterday by the way."

"Oh, thanks, did you watch?"

"Of course! When do I ever miss a match? Great all-round performance."

"Yep, cool to start with a win."

"Oh, and try and stay awake today, Danai!" Mr Stevens gave him a knowing grin.

Danai just crumbled with embarrassment and fumbled a few words of contrition.

He was disappointed to see no note on the seat, or on the table. Tee must have forgotten. He felt crushed. This *really* must be how love felt. When he sat down though he noticed a small piece of paper wedged between the table top and the metal frame. He pulled it out and carefully unfolded it, as if he was a forensics expert, not wanting to cause any damage to the paper.

Yo, Danai!

Hope you see this note. Boring lesson today, all theory. The answer to the first multiple-choice question is A. Can't remember the rest. Noom is being a fool, trying to get Stevens to talk about random stuff. Usual Noom. Better go, think he can see I'm not writing notes in my book!

Have a good lesson buddy!

Captain Tee 555

He felt amazing. Of course there was no confession of love, it was basically a nothingy chit-chat note. But… but, the guy he had been obsessed with for ages had written him a secret note. A secret note. You didn't leave secret notes for just anyone, did you? He carefully folded the note and put it in the back of his school diary for safe keeping.

He didn't fall asleep, but he did spend another lesson in something of a daydream. Though he did correctly volunteer the answer to the first multiple-choice question.

TWELVE

It was a common Friday routine for Danai and Noom to hang out in the Silom Complex after school and then go back to Danai's place for some dinner and just chilling out, with Noom often sleeping over. Sometimes they'd be a bigger Friday night out, with a group of them going out usually to a movie, or bowling or a restaurant. They weren't really too heavily into the party scene; of the style they'd seen so much of in American movies. It certainly wasn't the case around their circle of friends anyway.

"Danoom! You going to the mall?" Golf shouted across the school courtyard. It always amused and pleased them when people referred to them as Danoom. They'd invested a lot of energy trying to get that nickname to take off in Grade Ten, and too few actually used it.

Noom turned and punched his arm in the air as Golf ran to catch up.

"So you want some final dating tips from Danoom?"

"Hello? What the fuck do either of you know about dating?" Golf put on a face of mock confusion.

"Why don't you ask Danai's mum later tonight?"

"Oh, for fuck's sake, enough with this shit!" Danai punched his mate on his arm.

The three of them slowly wandered away from school, chatting and bantering as they went. The number of times they stopped to exclaim amazement at what had been said or to loiter by a shop it was astonishing how long it could take them to cover the short distance.

"Where's Tee?" Danai tried to ask normally, but he was self-conscious, worried that he sounded like someone who desperately wanted to know.

Golf crudely signalled with his index finger and fist exactly what he thought Tee and Fern might be doing.

Noom laughed and Danai joined him, though inside hoping it wasn't true. He slipped back into his daydream as Golf and Noom carried on talking nonsense.

Maybe he's with Fern, just as a friend. Maybe he's talking to her right now about how much he really loves me. Maybe he thinks the same as me and neither of us know the other thinks the same.

The walk from BSIS to Silom Complex took them down a couple of small side roads and into Sala Daeng Road before coming out on Silom Road by the mall. At a normal pace it was about a ten-minute walk, leaving school on a Friday it could easily take twenty-five minutes. It was a short walk that encapsulated modern Thailand. Between the high-rise office blocks on Sathorn Road and those on Silom Road; intermingled with malls and shops, followed by the shortcut through small streets which still retained an old Thai feel. Shop houses, a few food stalls, quiet residential buildings and even some small old-style businesses. They stopped off at the regular fruit and drinks stall, the woman who ran the stall was about sixty, to the boys she was about a hundred. She was always super friendly and in particular took a shine to Noom and Danai, who were always so polite.

"My favourite two boys!" she shouted as she saw them approach from over the road. She loved how they'd both chat to her using respectful language, but also with a tinge of informality and jokes.

"Two pomegranate juice, please," Danai ordered as she waved her arm.

"You don't need to order unless it changes! Same always!" She grinned at the boys.

"You know us too well." Noom wiped the sweat off his brow. "We're going to the mall to advise our friend about his date tomorrow!"

Golf grinned. "Come on, I don't need advice. I'm smooth."

"So you'll pay for her, yes?" Miss Malee asked.

"No! It's the twenty-first century."

"OK, boys. He needs your help. Show him how to be polite. Yes?" She directed her words to Danai.

"Impossible! We've been trying for years!" Danai laughed as he handed her the cash and took the two drinks.

Danai and Noom had particularly won the admiration and respect of Miss Malee when the previous New Year holiday they had given her a small pack of luxury cookies on the last day of term. She gave them a big hug. The school kids were a big part of her afternoon business and generally they were polite, but Noom and Danai stood out above the crowd.

"Thanks so much, Malee, see you next week!"

She waved the boys away and was already dealing with her next customer.

"You boys treat that old woman like she's your grandmother."

"She's a legend!" Danai and Noom said in unison, before high-fiving each other. Golf shook his head in bemusement.

"So what does Beem think about Nice? He got any advice for you?"

Golf began laughing even before Noom had finished the question. "Come on? He's my best mate, but love advice? He knows nothing!"

"That's not true, he has a bigger love than any of us," Danai spoke in a serious tone.

"What?"

"His putter!"

"Shows what you know, his favourite club is his 5-iron, apparently."

It amused Golf that he was saying this. Beem would be so impressed. Golf usually feigned boredom when it came to golf chat, sticking to his stock lines of "Let's talk about the real Golf!" pointing to his chest. Beem would be touched to know how much his friend actually listened and cared.

On a weekend they'd always head to one of the malls around Siam, but after school, Silom worked. It was never too busy and they had a big range of cafés on the lower floors. It was a stone's throw from the gay bars of Silom Soi 4 as well as the boy gogo-dancing bars of Soi Twilight and the infamous Patpong where some of Bangkok's tackiest ping pong shows took place. It meant there were often some interesting characters to be seen in the mall, just before a busy night of work.

The boys decided to go to a popular Korean fried chicken restaurant that was a regular haunt of most of them.

"Shit which one do I usually get, D? Spicy? Extra-spicy? Is it the crispier one?"

"What am I, your mum?"

"Oh, talking of mums—"

Danai quickly interrupted, "It's the spicy with Korean sauce you like."

Noom blew him a kiss.

"Fuck's sake, kids…Oh, pretty waitress. Let me order." Golf liked to act the most mature of the trio and tried his best to sound it for the waitress. She took their order and walked off.

"Yeah, another one who likes a bit of Golf."

Noom and Danai laughed and shock their heads.

"So, Golf, about Nutt. You agree he's into Danai?"

"Oh, this again, Noom. Nutt? Nutt! He ain't in to anyone like that and even if he was…"

Danai tried in vain to stop the conversation. "Hmm. That is interesting actually." Golf put his hand on his chin and was deep in thought.

The waitress came back and brought them their drinks.

"Thanks, you're so kind." Golf winked at her, she barely noticed. He turned back to his friends. "You know what, Noom may have a point. He spoke about you a lot during that football match."

"That's cos I was so good!"

"I mean a lot! Like it was all, Danai's doing well, pass it to Danai, nice run Danai. He doesn't know anything about football. So I guess what he really meant was, 'nice legs' and 'ooh cute butt'."

Noom took over. "So we're agreed, the big question. Are you interested?"

Danai hesitated for a second. "Nutt? Nah, come on, it's Nutt."

"You hesitated, D, you hesitated!"

"You did hesitate," Golf added, nodding knowingly.

Later that evening Noom and Danai were lying back on Danai's bed looking at their phones. Catching up on TikTok and mindlessly looking through Instagram.

"So what you gonna do about Nutt?" He spoke so fast that his words were almost slurred.

"I am not going to do anything about Nutt! Come on, Noom." He shook his head while laughing.

"Oh, I nearly forgot." Noom had a glint in his eye.

"Forgot what?"

"Don't make out like you don't know."

"What you on about?" Danai screwed his face up.

"Make out, get it?" Noom laughed hysterically at his own joke. "I'm serious you need to be ready for Nutt, I can teach you how to kiss."

"What the actual fuck? Like you'd know."

"OK, good point, that's why we gotta practice."

"Noom, we are not thirteen-year-old girls!"

"That's sexist man." He shook his head in an exaggerated manner.

After a moment of silence, Noom lent in and kissed his best friend on the lips, just a small peck which he held for a second. Neither spoke for what seemed like ages.

"That was just to get you ready."

Danai had been slightly shocked when he felt his friend's lips on his, and slightly aroused, which weirded him out.

The second time Noom lent forward slowly and brought his lips to Danai's. He slowly pushed his tongue into his friend's mouth. Danai was lost in the moment and responded. For maybe ten seconds or so their tongues intertwined. Danai felt his erection grow, pressing against his school trousers.

Noom lay back on the bed and didn't say anything. They both looked up at the ceiling, Danai tried not to draw attention to the bulge in his trousers, hoping it would go away and his friend wouldn't notice.

"Nutt's a lucky guy, you kiss well man."

"Really? It's weird. What are we doing, we're best friends."

"Yeah, exactly, just friends. It's nothing. Though, that isn't." He pointed to the bulge in Danai's trousers.

"That's not cos of you. That's just a reaction."

Noom laughed. "Yeah I guess."

"You probably not seen one that big." They both laughed, which eased the awkwardness a bit.

"I'm serious, though, D, you're cute. Too cute for Nutt, but you can use him to you know, get some…"

Danai sat quietly before adding, "Maybe."

Later that evening when they went to bed, Noom fell asleep quickly, Danai lay in bed for ages wondering what he had done, worrying that his friendship with his closest mate was going to be damaged. Worried that Noom would think he was attracted to him, just because he got hard. He even questioned himself.

Am I attracted to my best friend?

He was confident that he wasn't, he even smiled to himself. Noom was no Tee in Danai's eyes. He took his phone one more time to check Instagram. Tee had added a couple of photos of his family dinner. Just of the food though unfortunately, no pics of the hottest smile in Bangkok.

They woke up on Saturday morning and acted like nothing had happened, which was a relief to them both. Noom lay on the sofa-bed that he'd slept on.

"What's the plan today, D-boy?"

"Fucked if I know. Siam One?"

"Original idea, that's why you're my best mate." He hurled a pillow which Danai skilfully evaded.

Siam One Mall around the Siam Skytrain station was a popular hangout for young people, particularly those with cash to spend and some of the wealthier students from the nearby Chulalongkorn University. There were plenty of cafés and restaurants to hang out in as well as a good range of clothing and technology shops to mindlessly browse. Danai and Noom had spent many a weekend there and although they were both bored of it at times, they tended just to head that way on auto pilot. The other big advantage was that there were other huge malls in the area, and the streets around Siam Square were great to just hang out in. As well as plenty of uni students. It was a constant theme of Noom's that they should try to date uni students, a few years their senior.

"We also need to get a strategy for Nutt," Noom spoke in a sincere tone.

"That sentence is wrong on so many levels…"

"Like what?"

"Err, like '*we*' and '*Nutt*' for starters." Danai laughed and threw the pillow back, Noom caught it in a flash.

"Bad news for you, D-boy, is that he is busy today. I just texted to see if he wanted to hang out."

"I'm going have to sleep with him to shut you up aren't I?"

Noom laughed. "Classic I am pressuring a friend to have sex with another friend!"

THIRTEEN

It was well after one when they finally were up and dressed and ready to leave the house. Danai having explained and argued with his mum that no they hadn't had breakfast and yes of course they'd have lunch out and no he didn't know what time he'd be back.

"Will you be joining us for dinner, Noom?"

"Oh, I can't tonight, gotta get back to my place sometime!"

As the front door closed he looked at Danai. "She definitely has a thing for me!"

Danai let it pass, it was technically true. Just not in the way his friend thought. Hoped. Joked.

Siam was as busy as ever, but they were skilled at slowly navigating their way through the crowds to get to Siam One. They had arranged to meet up with Tee and Fern and whoever else was around. It was always a pretty loose arrangement and tended to involve lots of updates on Line, working out who was in that part of town. Golf was keeping the exact location of his date with Nice a secret. The last thing he wanted was a bunch of his friends to be gawping at him. Beem was always playing golf on a Saturday and hanging around shopping malls was not really Nutt's thing. He'd always moan that Siam was too busy and not for him. They'd usually only see him at weekends if they went somewhere quieter.

They chose a popular noodle restaurant which also specialised in some of the food from the Isan region in the North East of Thailand. It was busy but they got a table, Fern and Tee joining them just after they had all sat down.

Danai gave a huge smile, as ever, when Tee was around. Tee looked typically hot and sexy, and unlike most they knew, he didn't need to put much effort in. It was a standing joke that Tee could just run his hand through his hair and it would look like he had spent an hour styling it.

"Fern, you are a lucky girl, this guy gets hotter every day!" Noom joked. Fern giggled. Danai tried hard not to blush.

"Come on! I'm just normal." He smiled and winked in Danai's general direction.

Danai imagined that it was a special, knowing wink just for him.

"So, I hear Nutt may have it bad for you?" Fern looked at Danai as she spoke. He nearly choked on his lunch.

"Noom! Is there anyone you haven't told this bullshit too?"

"Yes, me. What's this? You and Nutt?" Tee looked serious, and Danai hoped that maybe he'd be upset. Maybe he'd be jealous.

"It's purely in his imagination. Nutt is, eek, you

know. He's Nutt. I mean yeah he's not ugly, but come on, guys! He's Nutt!"

"He's not good enough for you D. Nutt's a nice guy. But you can do much better. I mean *soooo* much better." Tee continued to take this issue very seriously.

"Anyway, so what about err, literally anything else. Fern, how's your brother doing?"

Her brother had recently broken his leg in a motorbike accident on the way to university, and was lucky that his injuries weren't considerably worse.

"Thanks, D. He's OK, using it to his advantage. He has us doing everything for him! You know what he's like." They did. Aum had been something of a legend at BSIS. When Danai and his friends were in Grade 8, Aum was head student, good at everything, but one of those people who could get away with doing very little. There was always a group of friends to help him out, he even had the teachers running around after him at times. "Not seen Aum for ages, the legend!" Noom had particularly looked up to him, imagining that one day he'd be as popular and trendy.

"Yeah, he thinks he's a legend, you're lucky you don't have to live with him!" Fern rolled her eyes. It had always amused her how all her friends had worshipped her brother. "Your bro is doing some study thing with him you know?" she asked Danai. His brother Beer was a year younger than Aum.

"Beer? Studying? Not often, but he'd probably try to work his way into Aum's group of friends. Aum is so much cooler than Beer."

"Anyway, Danai, take it easy with Nutt, you don't have to listen to these guys, just…" She paused for dramatic effect and put both hands to her chest in a heart shape. "Listen here…"

The boys laughed at the cheesiness.

"Listen, boys, I gotta go and meet Ploy. She wants me to help her choose clothes. Enjoy chatting about football or whatever."

They waved her off. Danai really liked Fern, but at the same time he was always really happy when she left. In his mind she was his rival for Tee's affection. In. His. Mind. His delusional, fantasising mind. What a fantasy. He momentarily begun to gaze at Tee's face and had to snap himself out of it.

"Right, Danai. You should be on Grindr. Let's get you some action!" Noom put his arm around his buddy as he spoke.

"Grindr? What's that?"

"It's the men-only version of Tinder, come on! You don't know that?" Tee winked again as he spoke.

What is it with all this winking? Does it mean something?

"Maybe I am just not as obsessed with sex as you lot."

"Oh, please. Don't tell me you don't want some action." Noom squeezed his leg which he theatrically pushed away.

The truth was, Danai was quite keen to meet someone and he loved that his friends were so keen to help him. He'd read lots about this online, even the straight men were fascinated by what gay guys got up to. All men were potentially up for a bit of man-on-man action, he had read that somewhere. Especially when alcohol was involved. Noom and Tee began to plan Danai's profile.

"He should choose that picture you took after

football training last week."

"Yes, good shout Tee, and cool to know you study my Instagram!"

"Well, yeah you can take some good photos."

"Are you hearing this, D-boy? Don't tell me Tee doesn't know Insta skills when he sees it."

Danai ignored him and focused on Tee. "That photo, I look all sweaty, no?"

"You look cute, and guys will find the sporty thing hot. Noom, agree?"

"Agree!"

Danai busied himself choosing the image for his profile, and key stats.

"What the fuck do I write about myself? Sixteen-year-old boy looking for a date?"

Noom laughed. "What the actual fuck? You are clueless! You don't say sixteen! Leave it to me." He typed away, and then showed Tee, who nodded, before passing the phone back.

Uni boy, up for anything.

It was Danai's turn to laugh. "Is that it? Fucking J K Rowling here!"

"Trust me. When have I let you down?"

It was true, Noom always had his back.

He quietly flicked through a few profiles; it was all quite intimidating. So many good-looking guys, some with topless pics and quite graphic profile language. He suddenly felt quite self-conscious as the approximate geographical location popped up. Unsurprisingly there was dozens of guys within a few hundred metres of them, some within twenty or so, which meant they might be in the same café. His phone quickly started buzzing. New young meat on the scene it seemed. Most were amazingly uninspiring.

Hi
Yo
You hot

Some got straight to the point.

Sex now?
You have place?

Plenty were also quite direct with exactly what they could be doing together. He wasn't ready to start replying, but carried on looking through the pics as Noom and Tee chatted about something random.

Danai considered himself quite mature for his age, even if he had no experience of sex and dating. The Grindr app freaked him out a bit though. He couldn't believe how open and direct most of the guys were. There seemed to be a whole language he wasn't aware of. He started to feel a bit self-conscious with Noom overseeing his every move, not to mention Tee being there. Tee! He began to daydream about seeing a profile for Tee. Totally ridiculous since Tee was literally sitting opposite him.

"Oh, holy shit!"

"What you done now?"

"This guy asked what I was into…so I said football, fifa, anime…"

Noom began to laugh, knowing what was coming next. "His reply?"

"Cute, but I mean sex."

"And you said…" It was Tee's turn to chip in.

"Nothing yet. I mean. I dunno. What the fuck do I say?"

"Tell him you are a cute young virgin, he'll love that."

"Keep your voice down Noom!"

"Let me see his pic D." Danai passed his phone across to Tee.

"He's quite cute, but you can do better!" Tee began scrolling through a few of the profiles.

"Oh my fucking god!"

He handed the phone back, leaving the screen open on one profile.

'British bloke, sporty and fit.'

"No way. Is it him?"

"Who?"

All three looked in shock. Danai quickly shut down the app.

Noom was laid back. "So what? Mr Jameson's gay. Big deal boys. You think he's the only gay teacher at school? You kids, so naïve."

"I don't care about that. He's on the app!"

"Yeah, well, men gots needs."

"Fuck you can be slow at times Noom, what if he saw my profile too."

"Oh. OH!"

"Yeah oh. Hey, what you mean by *that* type of, 'oh'?" Danai tilted his head quizzically.

"You like Jameson! He's fit I guess for an older guy!"

The three of them chatted, gossiped. Danai laughed off the absurd suggestion that he might date a teacher. Not to mention that it was probably illegal.

They all reckoned Jameson wouldn't say anything, even if he had seen Danai's profile, on the basis that he wouldn't want to have people gossiping about him. Not to mention his topless profile picture.

Tee left to catch up with Fern, although he didn't seem to be that excited by it. It always gave Danai a little sinking feeling. The reminder that Tee had a girlfriend.

Noom smiled at his best mate. "My boy Danai got it bad."

"For fuck's sake, I'm not interested in Mr Jameson. At all!"

"Ha-ha. You know full well that I am talking about Tee."

"Oh…" He couldn't even add any kind of protest, and after a few seconds he knew it was too late to try and argue.

"Don't worry, even straight boys want Tee. I mean, he's perfection."

For a moment there was an awkward silence, something that never happened with the two of them.

"How did you know?"

"I know you. I can read your every look, but it's soooo obvious man. Your face lights up when he's around!"

"Fuck, does everyone know?"

"Well nah I mean it's obvious to me, but not everyone is a Danai Paratanatapoon expert!"

They talked about Tee, Danai confessing the extent of his love and obsession.

"It's obvious to you huh? It's not just his looks you know. I mean he's so nice. Thoughtful, caring…" He tailed off.

"I get it, dude. Tee makes us all look like losers!" Noom added "Well you never know what might happen, he won't be with Fern forever."

Danai smiled. He'd had this daydream many times. It was false hope, but that was Noom, always saw the positive.

"Never say never. Wonder if he kisses like me though…" His mouth opened, trying to be sensual but it ended in a full bellowing laugh.

"That," Danai said in mock anger, "is not meant to be discussed, ever!"

FOURTEEN

John Jameson had been shocked to see Danai's profile on Grindr, not shocked that a student was gay, but just shocked at seeing a student in an app that was predominantly used for people to meet for casual sex dates. He blocked Danai and hoped that the youngster hadn't seen him there. John had a very relaxed attitude to being 'out' at work, and even on occasions among students. What he didn't want was to become a focal point of rumours and gossiping. He had immediately picked up a strongly negative, almost certainly homophobic vibe from Allison Waugh and the last thing he wanted was for her to overhear students discussing seeing their coach on a gay dating app. She'd quickly twist the tale. It's often said that gay people have a 'gaydar', John always felt that his homophobe-radar was stronger. Straight people never got it, how one could so quickly and accurately judge someone. There were tell-tale signs, comments, looks. John was never wrong. His gaydar was often wrong, he had a policy of assuming everyone was gay until they proved otherwise, but his homophobe-radar was always spot on.

On another level he was really pleased to see Danai's profile there. It was always nice to find young people with that sort of confidence about their sexuality. John had never been open when he was a teen at school, the idea was crazy. Even his closest friends didn't know until he was in his twenties. If Danai *had* seen his profile then he hoped that he'd see his football coach as someone he could confide in. Danai was young, obviously naïve and impressionable, and someone needed to warn him about the sort of characters he might meet on dating apps. John had especially liked the idea of championing the position of gay role model in school sport. Even in the 21st century people had ludicrous stereotypes in their minds about what a gay man was. Sporty, school football coach, was rarely it.

"Hey, John! Sawatdii Khrap," Bank spoke with a beautifully clear voice as befitted someone who worked in media and PR, not effeminate, but yeah he did get closer to a stereotype. He sat down opposite John.

"Hi, Bank, Hugo Boss? Nice."

"Gotta keep the look fresh and young! Need a coffee?"

Bank was something of a shopaholic, he was in his early thirties but could probably pass for a uni student, and he still had a youthful exuberance. John had met him soon after arriving in Bangkok and they'd quickly become good friends. On one evening early in their friendship they'd had a few too many drinks and John wondered if they'd end up in bed.

They didn't, and with hindsight they were both happy about that. If they had, it was unlikely they'd have become such good friends. More likely they'd have become casual fuck-buddies and then slowly drifted until they had no contact.

"What's new? How's the new school?"

"Yeah, it's great so far. Just had a bit of a dilemma actually..."

"Ooh, hot gossip! What's his name?"

"No, not that kind of gossip. Was just on Grindr, and..."

"John, please! I don't need to know about your sordid hookups. Actually, I do. Tell tell..."

"Nothing like that, come on I'm meeting you for afternoon coffee! What you take me for? No, it's just I saw a student's profile there!"

"OK. I get it. Right. It's simple then. No, John, you cannot fuck one of your students. Honestly, it's obvious. You have to wait until he leaves school!" Bank smiled and winked at his mate.

"Behave, Bank! I'm serious. Do I speak to him about it?"

"Is he cute?" Bank's grin became mischievous.

"He's sixteen!"

"I didn't ask that—"

"He's a sixteen-year-old football player, of course he's cute! But think about all those old perverts circling him on that app."

"Not everyone's like you, John!"

"Hey... I'm not old!"

They laughed and eventually Bank did take the predicament seriously, for all the joking about cute young guys he realised it was an awkward position for a teacher to be in. His advice was sound, do nothing.

If the kid wants to chat, then great. If not, leave it, but keep an eye on him as a good teacher should. Jameson agreed.

Golf was amazed how well the chat flowed with Nice. He'd been really nervous, though of course he hadn't let his friends know that. With them he was all bravado, 'just a date.' But in reality he had been terrified. What if he ran out of things to say? That was his biggest fear, awkward silence and desperately trying to make small talk. Within ten minutes he was totally relaxed and chatting just as he would with any of his friends. The next panic went through his head. Does this mean we're meeting as friends, and not a date? Nice was into Korean Boy bands, something Golf knew little about. He was happy to let her chat away about the latest ins and outs and he promised to listen to some of her favourites.

"Maybe I should do my hair in Korean style?" Golf smiled, an attempt to flirt and establish what she thought about him.

"Cute! Don't though, your hair already looks cute. Different from the Korean cute. You have Thai cute!" She laughed.

"Oh, I'm cute. You're so kind!"

"I bet you are one of those guys who looks in the mirror all day telling yourself how cute you are!"

"How did you know? You seen me?" He grinned. "I'm surely the cutest guy in school, and do not mention Tee!" Even students from other international schools were aware of the legend that was Tee.

"Tee? Tee? Oh, Tee, is he hot? I hadn't noticed. Tee's just a bit too perfect, maybe he's a serial killer?"

"Imagine! Bangkok's cutest ever serial killer, kills with his smile."

"Oh, Golf, that is lame! Hey, is it wrong to make jokes about serial killers. I mean, that's bad right?"

"Hmm, I think it probably is!" Golf began to laugh a lot, and then was embarrassed at how much he laughed.

Nice was quick to mock. "Maybe not so cute when you got bubble tea dripping out your mouth."

The date was going great. He suggested going for lunch, she said yes. They had only planned going for coffee. Noom had said beforehand if you can extend the date beyond coffee then you are in! He started to wonder what it would be like to kiss her. He felt himself getting hard at the thought. He subtly moved his legs a bit, trying to adjust himself to become more comfortable. He decided he'd better focus on what Nice was saying, rather than imagining their lips touching.

"So who was that guy I saw you with last week? I thought you guys might be on a date…" Golf continued to try and establish what this coffee and lunch meant.

"Petch! So funny. Petch's one of my best friends."

"Just friend, eh?" Golf winked.

"Put it this way, he told me he'd date you if I didn't."

"Wow, so everyone thinks Golf is cute!" he tried to lean back with an arrogant and smug grin while nodding his head.

"But then he added that your friend is cuter than you, sorry."

"What? Beem?! How dare Petch say that. Beem is NOT cuter than me. Come on, let's not be silly now!"

"Sorry, Petch thinks so. Is Beem single?"

"Oh yes, very single."

"What does that mean?"

"Well he is in love, with golf. I mean really in love."

"With you? So he *does* like guys, Petch will be happy to hear."

Golf was already shaking his head. "No, I mean golf. Not Golf. The game. Golf is his life. He's not interested in dating anyone! He's obsessed with golf. That's it."

"Oh ok. So I will tell Petch to start playing golf, then we can go on double dates."

"So we *are* on a date?" Golf felt relaxed enough to joke about it.

"Yes. We definitely are."

He liked the way Nice was so assertive, she made it really easy for him. He didn't have to guess; the way guys did in movies. She liked him, that was clear. They were on a date. They'd go on another date.

He started to think about losing his virginity with Nice, and instantly got hard again. He panicked as they were about to leave the café and move to a restaurant. He had no control over it, and his jeans were quite tight. It'd be noticeable. They stood up and he managed to hold his hands in front of his crotch as they walked, and luckily his hard-on quickly receded. Girls were sooo lucky not to have this problem, he thought to himself.

Nutt sat in his bedroom and finished his maths homework. He excelled in maths and was enjoying Grade 11, as it was becoming more challenging. He was disappointed that this particular homework had been too easy. He'd have to comment to his teacher. He flicked through his Instagram feed, checking some of his favourite groups. 'Bangkok International School Cute Boys' was one of his favourites. Some of his school's students got on there. It was always a great badge of honour if someone submitted your photo to the group. He was excited to see a new photo of Danai. It was taken during a football match and he was wiping the sweat from his forehead. Noom had commented "My boy Danai! Hot AF!" The photo was steadily accumulating likes. Nutt wished he could like it multiple times. One really camp-looking guy had written "I want to eat him! Adorable!"

Noom had replied, to Danai's irritation. "Come get him, he's single!"

The next reply was "He likes boys lor?" To that Noom had just winked back, followed by Danai sending a few yawn emojis, and privately some expletives to his friend.

Nutt had had a crush on Danai since primary school, at that time he just didn't realise it was a crush. By the time he reached secondary school he realised he was into guys and specifically Danai. No one ever asked him anything about dating. Everyone just assumed that nerdy Nutt was only into maths and science and studying. He had started meeting guys from the internet when he was in Grade 10, and lied about his age. He was sure his mates would be amazed to know that he wasn't a virgin. He had one online friend who had become like a mentor to him. Ton was twenty-six and happy to just chat. It was refreshing for Nutt that there was one guy there who didn't want to just get him in bed. He sent Ton a screenshot of Danai's photo.

OMG! This is Danai! He IS cute!

Yes, I want him so bad Ton, what should I do?

First. Take your hand off it! Now!

Nutt laughed and cheekily replied, too late, just finished doing that.

They chatted mindlessly for a while, about school, work. Nutt quickly brought the conversation back to Danai. Ton's advice was blunt and to the point.

So isn't it time you just tell Danai how you feel?

Yeah, but, I don't wanna lose what I have with him now.

Nutt thought about this a lot. He'd rather be Danai's friend and see him often than risk saying something and making it weird and then they drift apart.

Ton had told him many times – that's life and love. We had to take risks at times.

Nutt sat backed and looked at his reflection in the mirror. He looked good. He didn't often think that of himself, maybe the lighting was just right today, but he was sure. He looked good. He know some people thought he looked stereotypically nerdy. He wore small glasses, and his hair was short with no particular style. His teeth certainly weren't perfect either, a little bit crooked on the bottom. But he had nice clear, soft skin and that was what he was sure made him look pretty good.

He texted Danai.

Any plans later D?

Nah. Noom has dinner with family. I'm feeling lazy to go out.

Wanna come over and hang here?

Nutt waited with anticipation, before Danai confirmed that he'd come round. Nutt felt a shiver of excitement. While there was nothing unusual about Danai at his place, this time he was determined to tell him how he felt.

He then sent him the same screenshot, casually adding 'nice pic'!

The reply was a sarcastic big kiss sticker. Nutt felt a reaction from his dick and began to daydream about kissing Danai, while softly rubbing it through his shorts.

Golf was feeling great after his lunch date. He was hoping to add a third phase, evening drinks with him and his friends. She had pre-empted his invite by saying she had to get home as her aunt was in town from Singapore. At the end of the date they agreed to go out again soon and quickly exchanged some Line messages after the date.

He texted Beem about their evening plans.

Drinks? Me, you, who else?

Whatever! Whoever! Where?

Demo?

Demo in Thong Lo was a regular club they visited. Golf had got to know some of the security guards there and was always generous with them. His group never even needed to show their fake ids.

He lay back on the bed, leaving a wet mark on the pillow from his hair, having just showered. He haphazardly shoved a towel under his head. He scrolled through Nice's Instagram pics, and then texted Tee for advice.

How many photos should I like? And how far back?

Tee just replied that he was crazy. Not very helpful.

He had to like *some* photos to show he was keen, but if he liked too many and went back too far it would suggest he was stalkerish. Which ones to like? Had to be the cutest ones. He had to set the right tone, send the right message.

He was naked on his bed, something he loved to do when he was alone at home. He felt such freedom. His dick got hard, especially from Nice's beach holiday photos. He slowly began to play with it. Something he'd been wanting to do since they were having coffee. Among his friendship group he was considered as being the one who had a bit of a success with girls. He was always keen on someone, always chatting up someone. The boys had just kinda assumed he was the most experienced, along with Tee. The truth was he'd got no further than a peck on the cheek and some hand holding. Beem knew this information, but Golf was happy to let the others think he was a legend with girls. In the same way they all 'just knew' Tee and Fern had gone all the way and were fucking. Sometimes Golf wondered if they were all just making the same assumption. He couldn't ask Tee though, he felt like if he did it would be admitting he was a virgin himself. Others said the fact that Tee was always coy and insisting he and Fern were just friends was the proof. The ones who brag were the liars. Tee's downplaying meant they were obviously fucking like rabbits!

It didn't take Golf long to finish, leaving a sticky mess on his chest that required a second quick shower. He jerked off at least once a day which he thought was pretty normal. Beem once confessed that he too jerked off, but maybe once a week or once every two weeks.

Golf was shocked. "What? Bullshit. I do it daily, sometimes more than once a day!"

"You fucking pervert!"

They argued over who was the freak, and both secretly worried about it. Beem had even googled it and the evidence suggested his infrequent jerking off made him more unusual.

Golf, Tee, and Beem arrived at Demo around 9pm. He warmly greeted A, the security guard and casually slipped some cash. It made him feel like some kinda mafia boss from a movie.

"Not out with Fern tonight?" Beem was always

softly spoken and to the point. He was a man of few words.

"Nah, think she's mad at me."

"Why? You want too much sex?" Golf was obsessed with the topic, he really wanted to know the truth.

"Just don't feel like being with her all the time. Anyway, it's more fun with you guys."

Beem nodded and Golf wandered off to get the drinks. He had stopped trying to persuade Beem to drink alcohol so he ordered two whisky and cokes, and one coke. Golf had sometimes overdone it and made himself sick from drinking too much. With Tee and Beem for company he'd be sensible. Tee would never really drink more than two or three drinks, enough to get merry but not properly drunk.

Danai picked up a vibe from Nutt's invite, in as much as a vibe could be picked up from a text. It wasn't quite his usual language. He had texted in 'karaoke language', which was in Thai but using the A-Z rather than Thai alphabet. They usually texted in English and spoke in Thai. Somehow it just felt different.

He texted Noom.

Nutt invited me over. Think he's gonna, err….

Ha-ha. He wants a bit of that hot bod. Maybe he saw the pic.

Err…

What?!

He did see it, he sent me a screenshot! Fuck!

Go D!

I can't date Nutt, can I?

Date? We all got needs man, rest your hand and let Nutt do the work!

Fuck off Noom!

Enjoy, D! Gotta go.

He added a big kiss and a sticker of a sexy guy posing.

Danai's pace was a bit quicker than normal as he ducked in the alley behind his house that served as a shortcut to Nutt's. The noodle stall on the corner was in full swing with all the red tables occupied. The old couple who ran it smiled warmly. He was a regular there, often his mum would send him to get noodles with pork and dumplings when she hadn't cooked for the family.

"Mee feern ru yang?" Miss Aoy muttered to him as he walked by. It was a standing joke, she always teased him, asking if he was dating anyone. She had insisted since he was about ten years old that he was too cute to be single. It was great that in Thai that the word for boyfriend/ girlfriend was the same, no different words for different genders. So any gay teens who weren't out, didn't need to lie.

He'd shout back that he had sooo many, while holding his thumb and forefinger to his face in a way that was a symbol of being cute in Thailand.

His thoughts were different though.

Maybe I'm off to meet my boyfriend now. Me and Nutt? Dating? Could we?

He laughed to himself at the idea that maybe he had totally misread Nutt's vibe. He arrived at Nutt's house and took a deep breath before ringing the doorbell.

"Yo Danai!"

Yo? That's definitely weird for Nutt. Is he nervous?

"Hey, looking sharp, man."

It was a sign, surely? Nutt was wearing polka dot shorts. Short shorts, and a tight t-shirt that showed off his slim figure. It looked new, and the Lacoste logo was sure to be genuine, knowing Nutt.

"Oh, thanks, I just bought these."

"Where are your parents tonight?"

"Some fancy dinner thingy with my mum's work."

"Party time!"

Nutt winked and smiled.

I've never seen Nutt wink. Ok, he's definitely flirting. Go with it Danai.

Nutt went straight upstairs, leading Danai to his bedroom. Again, not unusual but now of course it seemed suggestive.

"Golf and Beem are going to Demo with Tee, you didn't want to go?" Nutt was hoping Danai would answer that he wanted to be alone with him!

"Nah, not in the mood today. Too tired."

"Tee seems bored with Fern these days." It was a throwaway comment from Nutt, Danai tried to remain cool.

"Maybe. Dunno."

Bored because he wants to be with me. Shit what am I thinking, I am meant to be on a date here. Wait, am I?

"What about you? Any dates? That hot insta pic gonna get you lots of offers."

They laughed, which broke the ice for a moment. There was a definite vibe in the air, both could sense it.

"Nah, no dating."

"Just date this." Nutt held out his palm and giggled nervously.

He wasn't sure how to read the look of shock on his friends face, so added an explanation. "I mean, use your hand, to jerk off. You know. Bad joke…"

"Yeah, I kinda got that!"

"Good, or did you think I meant you should hold my hand?"

Danai didn't know how to respond to that. This was going quicker than he had anticipated. He sat awkwardly and smiled.

"Well, maybe it's a good idea?" Nutt was getting bolder.

"Dunno. I guess."

It felt like a slightly pathetic response, but he also felt it was perfect in the situation. It meant nothing, but could mean anything, or everything.

"Well, OK, that's not a no then. You know how

hot you are, D."

He blushed. "Me? Come on, I'm normal."

"That just makes you even hotter." He bravely rested his hand on Danai's thigh and was sure he noticed a slight bulge in the crotch area. He gently squeezed and then turned his hand over, inviting it to be held. Danai responded.

They sat in silence, their hands intertwined, slowly and sensually stroking each other with a finger. The silence was strong and vivid, making it an intense moment. Their eyes were locked but neither spoke for a minute or two.

"I feel like this is when we should kiss." Nutt broke the silence.

Danai's eyebrows arched upwards, but he was delighted by this boldness. He'd never have been brave enough to take the lead like this. His vagueness seemed to be working well.

"Yeah…"

Nutt leaned in clumsily and tried to kiss before realising that he should remove his glasses. They giggled. As soon as he felt Nutt's lips on his and then Nutt's tongue slowly push its way into his mouth, Danai's dick was throbbing to the max. Their tongues explored each other's mouths. It felt amazing though Danai felt he had no clue what he was doing. This was nothing like his kiss with Noom. Within minutes they were lying on the bed with Nutt on top trying to eat his friend's mouth. They could feel their dicks pressing through their shorts.

"Fuck I need you, Danai. I want to lick you all over."

He was breathless and began to strip off his clothes. Danai watched with fascination. This was nothing like watching porn online, this was so much more exciting. He made an audible moan as Nutt's dick popped out. It seemed huge to Danai, longer and thicker than his own.

"You like that? Don't be shy, baby." He helped Danai take his clothes off and they hugged each other close, rubbing their rock-hard dicks against their bodies.

He whimpered in shock as Nutt's mouth made its way between his legs and he took his dick into his mouth. It felt amazing. He clumsily tried to jerk Nutt off as he was being given an amazing blow job. He had no idea it would feel quite this good. Neither lasted long. They both lay back panting, covered in a sticky mess. It felt like a long intense sex session. It had lasted a little over five minutes.

"Wow, fuck. That was amazing. I'm exhausted." It was the most coherent Danai had been.

"You are so fucking hot." Nutt stroked his friend's stomach, playing with his cum.

"Yuck. Too messy!" They laughed and Nutt handed his new lover some tissues. He could sense he felt a bit exposed now in his nakedness. Danai went to the shower and emerged in a towel.

Nutt smiled at him. "Fuck your body is so amazing."

"Go and shower!" Danai shifted around, he wanted to take the towel off to dry and get dressed. With Nutt in the shower he texted Noom.

Gotta talk as soon as I get home. Yeah, Nutt is defo into me!

He followed it with a winking emoji.

FIFTEEN

Golf made sure the drinks were flowing, if not to get his friends drunk then to ensure he was drunk himself. He wanted to get their advice.

"Lots of hot girls in here tonight." Neither friend reacted.

"Any hot ones for you Beemer?"

Beem shrugged, Tee laughed. "Thought you were into Nice?"

"Yeah, I am man. I mean really into her. On the date I had to keep rearranging my boxers."

This time Beem almost scowled, it was amazing how often Golf talked about jerking off, or his dick generally.

"Too much info, dude." Tee sipped from his Jack and Coke. Tee was always careful when he was drinking. He drank slowly and liked to dilute his drinks with lots of coke. Like many of his friends he had a propensity to get red in the face when he drank alcohol. He had learnt how to moderate the effects of 'Asian Flush' with plenty of soft drinks and not overdoing the alcohol.

"I think I need your advice, Tee."

"Me? Sure, what you wanna know? Second date, where to go?"

"Dinner." Beem chipped in with a rare thought.

"Nah, too cheesy. Something more chilled, JJ market or that new mall down near Thong Lo." Tee corrected Beem.

"And then Bonchon?"

"Now you with it Beem, love Bonchon!"

Everyone loved Bonchon. The Korean fried chicken chain was popular among old and young alike, the menu was simple and the food delicious.

"Bonchon tomorrow?" Tee and Beem high-fived.

"No! Listen!"

They both looked at Golf. Tee put on a concerned voice "You're not interested in Bonchon tomorrow?"

"When have I ever said no to Bonchon? I mean that ain't what I want advice about. Geez." Golf shifted around as he took a few swigs from his drink.

"So, what then?" Tee continued to drink very slowly. If he emptied his drink too soon then Golf would just top it up and he'd drink too much, too quickly.

"You know…" he gesticulated by raising his eyebrows.

"No, we don't." Tee looked blank.

"Clearly." He sighed. "Sex! For fuck's sake! Sex."

"Oh here we go, not the jerking off thing again." Beem became more animated, it had been on his mind. He hadn't jerked off for over a week, and was now worrying he was abnormal.

"Not sex alone, Beemer!"

Tee just looked blank. "So…"

"I think I want to have sex with Nice. I mean, if she's keen, she seems to like me."

"Don't drug her!"

"Beem, I'm serious. I mean, I dunno, whatevs."

"You mean, you want advice about actual sex?" The penny had finally dropped for Tee.

"Halle-fucking-lujah"

"You've got enough experience, every day," Beem added.

"Yeah, but my hand and I have been going steady for years!"

"We talking first time then?" Tee was now getting serious. Golf just nodded.

Tee put his hand on Golf's shoulder, a calming 'leave it to me' vibe. "OK, so what advice you want?"

"Well, I dunno. Your first time with Fern. How was it?"

"Errr…"

"Don't get shy on me now, man. I'm opening up to you here. I mean, who started it? Did you just kiss her? Touch her? Did you discuss and plan it with her in advance?"

"Umm…" Tee wasn't often lost for words.

Beem was now quite fascinated, observing the deep intensity of his friends' conversation.

"Golf…"

"Yeah?"

"It's kinda complicated."

"Tee, just tell us. It's only the three of us here, we won't gossip."

"Nothing to tell."

"Oh, come on, dude. You must remember."

"I mean, nothing to remember."

Golf waved his arm, dismissively. It was then Tee's

turn to open up.

"No one believes me. Fuck you guys. I've never had sex with Fern. OK!"

Beem's jaw dropped. "What the actual fuck."

"Are you shitting me?" Golf wasn't sure what he felt about this revelation.

"I told you, it's complicated. She wants to do it, but I dunno. I just don't get the same vibe."

"Fuck, you're as bad as Beem. He doesn't even jerk off."

Beem went red. Tee just laughed.

"So, let me get this straight. The hottest girl in school wants to have sex with you, and you said no?"

"Pretty much. Is that weird?" Tee was showing an insecurity that his friends had never seen before.

"No, it's not weird." Beem tried to assert himself before Golf just spoke over him. "Yes, it's fucking weird. I mean super weird. I'd get hard if she even smiled at me!"

"It's like, she's a good friend. We've been dating for years. I like just hanging out with her."

"Wait. So what do you guys do? She jerk you off? You, touch her?"

"Nothing. We are just friends, like us!"

"I'm shocked."

"Even, I am fucking shocked." This was Beem at his most animated.

"See that Tee, now you've even got little sweet Beemy swearing! What is going on? I'm a virgin, Tee's a virgin. What next, we gonna find out that Beem's been fucking for years?"

"You got me!" He laughed. "Nah, I'm still that guy who jerks off like once every two weeks."

"Wait. This jerk-off thing is real?" Tee was now

genuinely surprised; he had assumed Golf was just bantering.

"OK, enough sex talk, boys! Wanna hear about my bunker shots today?"

"Well, then we need a lot more of this!" Golf poured a big slug of JD into his glass and topped it up with a little splash of coke.

Golf was feeling a mixture of confused and intrigued, and happy. He always assumed he was the one lagging behind a bit, in the dating and sex stakes. Yet to find out that the school stud Tee was, not just a virgin, but doing nothing at all with his girlfriend was quite the revelation. Maybe all the guys at school were exaggerating about their sex lives. Maybe Beem was quietly the one getting all the action. That point made him grin, no chance. Beem could look at photos of golf clubs or some golfer playing a shot and have the same reaction as Golf would looking at a bikini-clad model.

They left the serious conversations and just enjoyed the rest of their evening. They didn't overdo the drinking and Golf returned the bottle to the bar. They had a system where they'd put a sticker with a number on the bottle and they could return to the bottle next time by showing their ID.

The three of them shared a taxi home, dropping Golf off before arriving at Tee's place. Beem got out with Tee as his house was just a short walk. They sat down on the bench in Tee's front yard.

"I didn't mean to mock you about the jerking off thing you know, guess I was just surprised."

"That's cool Tee. Is it really that weird? Golf seems to be shocked!"

"It's not weird. I'm the same you know. Don't do it much. Maybe we are both weird then."

Beem laughed. "I mean I like it. It feels good. But I just don't need to do that all the time. Eating pizza feels good too!"

It was Tee's turn to laugh. "Now pizza I *could* do every day!"

Beem looked at him. "You are going a bit red there Tee."

"Yeah, I can feel it a bit. I try to be so careful drinking, or I'd go bright red and get hot, fast."

"Enough about how hot you are!"

They chatted a bit longer about this and that, golf and Golf. Tee had never really had a deep chat like this with Beem. He gave him a warm, slightly drunken hug before Beem slowly walked the few minutes back to his home.

SIXTEEN

John Jameson had put 'Grindrgate' out of his mind until the moment he walked into school and saw Noom and Danai quietly chatting in the corner of the school's outdoor atrium. He suddenly wondered if he needed to prepare himself to be the topic of student gossip. He could do without that hassle.

"Morning boys, good weekend?"

"Of course. It's the weekend!" Noom spoke on behalf of them both.

"I hope you are both well rested for the big game this week."

"Professionals are always ready." Danai thumped his chest.

John tried to see if he could detect any sort of look of embarrassment in Danai. Nothing obvious. Maybe he hadn't seen his coach's profile after all.

"Oh, coach. One thing. Might be an idea to play D more central in this game, let his pace attack the middle of their defence, they are weak there." Noom was confidently getting into his stride.

"I see. You've been scouting Lad Phrao International School have you?" John titled his head, eyes widening.

"Always got my people keeping an eye on things coach."

"Great. It might be an idea for me to give you a rest on the bench. You know, we don't want anyone getting too cocky that they think they can tell the coach what team to pick…" John spoke with a strong hint of sarcasm, Noom got the hint.

Danai lightly punched his mate on his upper arm.

"Woah! Point taken, Coach Jameson, sir. I mean, you know best, of course, forget I said anything."

"I know best. You know I think that might just be the smartest thing I've ever heard you say."

"Oooh harsh, Jamo! Burnt, Noom man, burnt!"

"Jamo?" John put on a semi-serious tone.

"Mr Jameson! Coach! You must have misheard me."

"Yes, I thought I must have."

John walked away convinced the boys behaviour was exactly the same as ever. He must have blocked Danai before he saw anything.

Once 'Jamo' was out of sight the boys began talking again.

"Err, Jamo? You flirting with coach now?"

"Fuck off! Anyway, he can't have seen my profile. He was totally normal."

"Yeah, maybe he just scans past the schoolboys!"

Danai laughed.

"Talking of cuties, what the fuck is going on with you and Nutt?"

"We chatted normally yesterday. I think we're dating, like officially. I'm going to his again after school."

"God damn it. You're fucking before me. This is total BS man."

"If you've got it, mate…" Danai was trying to get cocky and did a cute smile and pose, like he was being photographed, with his thumb and index finger held under his chin.

"So, no denial! You are actually, you know, I mean, Jesus. Did it hurt? Can you sit down?"

The next punch from Danai was a bit harder. "Perv. We didn't actually do *that.* Fuck, I don't know about that yet."

"So, what did you do?"

"Whatevers, you know."

"Don't get shy on me now! I don't fucking know. Suddenly my best mate is on apps, dating guys. So, he gave you a BJ?"

Danai blushed.

"Oh, my god, he did. Was it good?"

"Well, yeah. He knows what he's doing."

"What the actual fuck! We're talking about Nutt? Nerdy maths geek Nutt!" Noom was a combination of excited with the gossip, but also shocked.

"Yeah, he said he met guys before. He dated an older guy last year."

"Jeez. You think you know people! So, one last question…"

"Noomster, haven't you asked enough questions?"

"Crucial one. Does he kiss better than me?"

The third punch was the hardest of the lot.

"Shit, D, you might actually hurt me if you get twice as powerful with your punches!"

"We are not meant to talk about that ever again, but, yeah he's better than you!"

Noom pretended to look upset. "Bullshit. You just don't want to admit that I'm the best, so yeah, let's not talk about it."

Nutt texted Danai just before he arrived at school.

Are we telling people?

Telling what?

That we're Grade 11's hottest couple!

Oh! No, I don't know. Are we?

Are we what?

Nutt was now worrying that Danai wasn't as keen as he was.

A couple…

Aren't we? Do you want to be? I do!

"Your bae texting?" Noom could tell from his friend's expression.

"He's asking if we are a couple!"

"What! Me and you?"

"Noom! This is serious."

"OK. OK. So say yes. Doesn't mean you're getting married. Just getting some action."

Yeah, I do too.

Nutt then sent a succession of hearts and cute stickers that was so out of character with his usual nerdy persona.

Danai followed with some messages telling his new boyfriend that it was too early for them to go public, but that Noom knew.

Minutes later Nutt walked towards them with a big grin on his face. He winked at Danai.

"You two better not starting acting like a pair of Grade 6 kids for fucks sake."

"Grade 6? Pedo!" Nutt laughed, it broke the ice and they got into normal school chat.

Miss Waugh skulked along, her hair slightly wet and matted with a scowl on her face. Her two sons walked deliberately a good few metres behind, desperate to avoid being seen walking in with their evil and hated mother.

She immediately barked in her high-pitched angry voice. "Err. Noom, and you, tuck your shirt in and put that phone away this minute or I will take it."

"It's not even the start of the school day yet Miss."

"How dare you talk back to me. Phone away now, or I'll lock it away for the week."

She skulked on; her shoulders slightly hunched. She had the gait of a comedy villain.

"What a fucking evil bitch." Noom spoke for them all. It was typical. She barely knew the names of students, even those supposedly in her care. The students could also tell that other teachers thought similarly about her.

Nutt whispered to his boyfriend, "I wanna hold your hand."

"Yeah, well you can. At my place after school."

Nutt didn't push it, the last thing he wanted was to push Danai away when everything seemed to be falling into place. There was a side of him that longed for them to be public, so that everyone would know the quiet kid they knew as the nerdy maths geek was dating one of the hottest members of the school football squad.

SEVENTEEN

At the end of the day, Noom and Danai walked out of school together, as was usually the case, with a plan to hang out in the in the Silom Centre Mall for a bit. It was why they basically enjoyed school, despite the boredom of some lessons and the pain in the ass of homework, it was also their social time. As older students they were allowed off the school campus for lunch, and they'd usually hang out for at least an hour at the end of the school day.

"Where's Nutt?" Noom asked with a suggestive wink.

"I dunno. I don't own him."

"So he's let you go out with me then."

"Fuck off Noom!"

"Just thought you might want to see him, that's all."

"I am. He's coming over later." Danai tried to sound matter of fact, and not to smile.

"Aha. You slag!" Noom continued to mock his best friend. "It's OK, D. I'm just jealous. I've only got my hand to date. Every day!"

"Yeah, I get it. I don't need to know all the details."

Monday was usually a football training day, but it had been cancelled due to some teacher meeting after school. The boys had complained to Mr Jameson that it was unacceptable and he'd agreed to a Tuesday training instead. They had a big match on Friday, and the team thought it was important they had a session to focus on tactics for the match. They needed to win against one of their big rivals to keep alive the dream of winning the league championship.

"Did you see Jamo again today?"

"Yeah, at break, he was on duty. I don't think he knows anything."

"Guess he didn't see your cutsie profile then."

They discussed the significance of seeing their football coach's profile, and torso pics.

"Maybe I should create my own profile." Noom had a cheeky grin as he spoke.

"What? Why?"

"Well, it's not fair you getting all this attention, and action."

Danai look wide-eyed and startled before his mate explained.

"Joking. I mean a fake one. Could chat with Jamo. See what his story is, maybe he has more revealing pics in private."

"Do you wanna see more revealing pics of Jamo?!" Danai turned the tables on his mate. Noom just laughed. "It sounds a bit dodgy that Noom. Isn't that illegal?"

Trust Danai to be so sensible.

"Anyway, if I want action, my best friend has a

lovely tongue."

Danai punched him, fairly hard, on his bicep.

"Ooh, baby D likes it rough, who knew?"

Before Danai could respond, Noom noticed Tee. Noom suddenly registered in his mind to find out whether Danai still had a thing for Tee, now he was getting together with Nutt.

Tee looked pensive, sad almost, as he absent-mindedly browsed a clothes shop.

"Tee!" Noom shouted to get his attention. Danai instantly turned his head to search.

Noom noticed and thought this confirmed that Danai was definitely not over Tee.

"Where's Fern?" Noom looked around as he spoke.

"With her friends. Think we probably breaking up."

"Shit buddy. You OK?" Noom put his hand on his mate's shoulder and gave him a gentle friendly rub.

Danai felt a rush of envy, wishing he had thought to do that.

Maybe I can give him a big warm hug.

"Danai?"

"Sorry Tee, was daydreaming."

"About the game this week?"

"Yeah, games. I'm sure." Noom chipped in. Danai gave him a gentle and subtle elbow to the ribs.

"Wanna go to Starbucks?" Danai gave Tee's shoulder a gentle squeeze. He immediately felt it seemed fake, contrived. Trust Noom to do it right.

He held his hand there for a second or two and tried to convince himself there was an energy, a moment.

Tee seemed to gaze into his eyes. "Thanks, yeah."

"D boy, I thought you had to go home?" Noom loved playing these sorts of games.

"Nah, not just yet. Let's go."

It amazed Danai that Tee seemed to be depressed, he didn't realise it was possible that someone as perfect as Tee could feel low.

As they were walking to Starbucks Danai sent Noom a Line message.

Don't tell Tee about Nutt!

He then nudged him to signal that he should check his phone.

OK. But maybe it would make him jealous?

Danai sent a couple of stickers in reply, one of mock anger and one of shock and confusion. Maybe Noom was right. He wondered if this was to become one of those movie storylines where the 'destined to be lovers' were never single at the same time.

Danai grabbed a table. "Sit down Tee, drinks are on Noomster."

"Fuck you! What ya want, Tee?"

He asked for a mango frappe, Noom already knew Danai's order.

Once Noom had gone to order, he dived straight in.

"So, really that bad with Fern?"

"Bad, well, wrong word really. I mean, I always told you guys we were just friends so, it's like ok."

"Yeah, sorry, we didn't actually believe that. We thought you were just being modest, shy, whatever."

"I don't want to actually be her boyfriend."

"So don't. Problem solved. It's only a big deal if you make it a big deal."

Tee smiled. Danai felt like he momentarily closed his eyes. Tee's smile could melt him. He wanted to shout, 'I love you, be with me.' Then he remembered he'd just started dating Nutt.

"That's it? Simple as that."

"Yes! Simple as. Gotta enjoy life, Tee. Too weird to see you sad, you're too cool for that."

"Thanks, Danai. You always know what to say."

"Me?" He was genuinely amazed, and felt a real sense of joy that Tee had noticed something like this.

He didn't know what to say. What was the correct response? He felt like it needed a subtle but flirtatious line. One that needn't be interpreted in a flirty way, but *could* be…

"One mango frappe, one cookies 'n' cream for my boy Danai."

Typical Noom, bursting back to the table just when he was having an emotional moment with Tee. Though he was also partly relieved as he hadn't thought up a good response.

"Danai says I am overthinking things and I should just break up with Fern."

"Oh, he does, does he?" Noom grinned at his best mate. "So this guy gives dating advice now? Still single, eh, D?"

"Yeah. Just the same as you."

"Sure about that?"

Danai kicked Noom under the table and he was sure he detected a sort of knowing nod from Tee.

Shit. Does he know? What does he think?

Danai actually wanted Tee to know. He wasn't

embarrassed or anything, it's just he wasn't entirely sure what he and Nutt were. But also he liked the idea that Tee might be jealous. If Tee didn't even know, then Danai couldn't cling to that daydream.

"Anyway, this time Danai is right. You should move on. You're the hottest guy in school. Take your pick mate."

Danai was quick to chirp back at him. "Take your pick? So fucking sexist Noom, and also, I think you'll find *I'm* the hottest guy in school. Verified by Instagram!"

"You, D, are the third hottest guy around this table. I mean, that hair. That's not even a style.

"Aww that's not fair, Danai's hair has its own style. Anyway, Nutt must like it." Tee grinned as he spoke. Noom did an exaggerated open mouth slack-jawed shocked expression.

"What the actual fuck. How do you know about me and Nutt?"

"Well, I didn't until just this second!"

Noom roared with laughter. "Classic. Oh, man."

"It's cool, D, Nutt's a lucky guy. I mean, you are defo the second hottest guy at this table!"

That smile. He was so beautiful, Danai just wanted to hold him. Touch him. Kiss him. Yet here he was talking about another guy he was apparently dating.

"How did you guess?"

"Come on, man. Nutt's been hanging around the team for ages. I mean. The way he stares at you."

"It's not really anything at the moment."

"This is surreal Tee. I'm single. You about to be single and shy cute little Danai's got himself a friend with benefits! Fuck, bruh."

They all laughed. Noom jokingly stroking Danai's

face.

"Anyway. You got a happy vibe about you today and I was sure I saw a little look between you and Nutt. I'm not stupid."

EIGHTEEN

Danai walked home with a mixture of excitement and nerves. Yes, he had got together with Nutt on their previous 'date' but what happened now? What was the process? Do they just kiss immediately and tear each other's clothes off? Or was that just a thing that happened in movies. He realised he didn't have a fucking clue what he was doing.

He also had a spring in his step from just spending time with Tee. He felt he had seen a different side to him, and realised that Tee knew him better than he had thought. Was he basically happy because Tee was breaking up with Fern? Was it shitty of him to try and encourage him? What did that say about him and Nutt? It was all so complicated.

It was a little after five pm, but evening was already setting in. There was a humid heat to Bangkok most times of the year. A stifling intensity. Danai was starting to sweat and wondered if he should wait for Nutt and suggest they shower together. Would that sound sleazy? Did couples shower together on their second date?

He texted Noom.

I don't have a clue what I'm doing. Me and Nutt. It's stupid!

Chill, D. Don't take it too seriously. Enjoy yourself.

Noom was right, even if his text wasn't much help. He decided to message Nutt and work out exactly what was gonna happen.

Nutt replied with a mischievous grin sticker.

I'm on my way. Wait. I'll shower with you!

That question was answered. It was handy that Nutt was more forward. They were going to shower together, so they were clearly going to have sex again. Danai was curious as to what else they'd try. It was hot what they'd done last time and he wasn't sure if he was ready to go that bit further. What if Nutt wanted to fuck him? Would it hurt? Did he want that? Did he want to fuck Nutt? He really didn't know. He had watched enough online porn to know it looked hot, but he wasn't quite sure about actually going about it himself.

Nutt arrived within ten minutes of their text exchange.

"Hey, babe."

Danai giggled. It didn't sound quite right to him, but he liked hearing it anyway.

"What's up, Nutt?"

"You, I hope!" He moved to kiss him, their lips

met and immediately Nutt pushed his tongue inside Danai's mouth. Danai wasn't quite ready for it but he quickly got into the flow. Nutt's mouth tasted so good. Minty. He'd clearly just brushed his teeth. They passionately explored each other's mouth in a horny frenzy.

They broke away from each other.

"You taste so fresh and minty. Sorry I didn't brush my teeth, let's go upstairs and I'll do it now."

"Relax, D baby. You taste amazing. I love your tongue."

They rushed upstairs. Nutt's hands intermittently squeezing Danai's tight ass on the way. As soon as they reached the bedroom Nutt began taking his clothes off.

Nutt stood there, butt naked and pulled his lover towards him. His hands explored under Danai's shirt as he began pushing his tongue back into his mouth. Danai could feel Nutt's hard dick pressing against him.

"Take your shirt off, I wanna see that hot bod." He broke off to speak, breathlessly, before pushing his tongue back.

Danai was relieved that Nutt was so confident, so sure of how this all worked.

"I wanna see your hard dick, babe." Nutt felt it through his trousers and Danai let out a small squeal of excitement. It felt so fucking good.

"OK, let's go to the shower. I'm too sweaty."

"Sexy!"

Nutt led the way to the shower, and then insisted Danai wait until the water temperature was just right. It was cute how caring Nutt was, seconds after he was raging with lust and horniness. Danai stood there, naked in his own bathroom, momentarily feeling slightly uncomfortable. Was he meant to cover up? Or maybe feel Nutt's sexy body as he adjusted the water temperature. He stood, waiting for his bae to take control.

"It's just right, like your cute body and hot dick."

Danai blushed and giggled. "baak waan na" literally it meant 'sweet mouth', for a guy who was a sweet talker.

"Yes, my mouth must taste sweet." Again, he pulled Danai towards him and instigated another wet, passionate kiss.

Danai wanted Nutt to suck him again, but didn't know how he should ask. He carried on kissing. Waiting for Nutt to take the lead. The kissing was so good, he loved the feel, but couldn't really explain why the taste was so good. Eventually Nutt got down on his knees and took his buddy's dick into his mouth.

"Wow, you got it all in." Danai was amazed, not because he thought his dick was big but he couldn't ever imagine having that skill himself.

"Fuck that feels so good. I'm gonna, err, soon. Fuck."

Nutt broke for a second to speak. "Do it, baby, whenever you want." He smiled, kissed Danai's dick and then began to frantically suck it again.

Danai couldn't believe how good it felt. Even better than last time. How could anything feel this good? I mean, yeah jerking off was one of the most awesome things any guy ever did, but this was something else. Was he meant to shoot in his buddy's mouth? Nutt's actions suggested that it was ok. Danai wanted to, so badly. As he got close he lost any control and instinctively put both hands on the back of Nutt's head. His body jerked as he shot his cum into his boyfriend's mouth. He immediately felt a bit embarrassed.

"Sorry. Sorry. Wow."

Nutt moaned and eventually pulled away, opening his mouth to show there was nothing there. "Awesome babe, fuck that was so hot."

"You swallowed! Sorry!"

"I wanted it, I love it baby."

He went in to kiss, but this time Danai shied away.

"Don't wanna taste it?" Nutt asked.

"Ew. That's weird."

"I don't mind. I love it. I love that it's you, in me."

Danai looked down at Nutt's hard dick. "You need to, you know…finish?"

"Yeah, suck my nipples, baby."

Danai had lost that feeling, but tried to get into it. Flicking his tongue around Nutt's chest.

It didn't take long, and he came with force against Danai's leg. They embraced, tired, all their energy sapped.

"That was so fucking hot, D. We better wash now."

NINETEEN

One of the big positives for John Jameson of working at BSIS was the location. He loved the area around Silom, and not for the stereotypically predictable reason that many gay men liked the area. Yes, it was true that on occasions John still enjoyed a night out in the gay bars of Soi 4, or even clubbing at the infamous DJ Station.

However, for John it was the whole mix he loved. There was a buzz. Lumpini Park was his go-to running spot, which had a great vibe before seven am. The area had shopping malls, great restaurants covering the full range of the Thai spectrum, and yeah there were bars, including the sketchy and sleazy ones, to suit all tastes. It was two stops on the Skytrain to Siam and the links to Sukhumvit and other parts of the city. In the other direction you could be by the river in ten minutes. John had a great apartment in a small side road, just off Sala Daeng Road. It was less than fifteen minutes' walk to work.

He'd arranged to meet his friend Bank for dinner

at the Silom Complex.

"Mwah mwah, how you doing John?"

"Classic. Enough with the fake pretentiousness, you know it's lost on me."

Bank always did exaggerated air kisses, just to irritate his mate.

"Ooh, sorry, I forgot. Macho sport man! Football!"

They both laughed. On the surface they had so little in common, but over the years they had become really close friends. Bank was that one person John could always call for a chat. He could be totally honest with Bank, whatever it was. Bank was unshockable and genuinely non-judgemental.

In his early years in Bangkok, John had certainly lived something of a hedonistic lifestyle. Drugs, sex, random hookups were all part of his typical weekly routine. As he hit his thirties he quickly realised that drugs and drink made it increasingly challenging to keep in shape, and since sport was so important to him, he simply stopped. He remembered amusingly telling Bank that he basically enjoyed football, running and swimming more than sex and drugs. It was logically simple. So he stopped doing any drugs, and went from too much binge drinking to just simple social drinking. Basically he just cut out all his excesses.

They sat down at a decent restaurant chain that they often visited.

"So, any dating with those cute students in your new school?"

"Bank…"

"Not even one? One quick BJ?"

"Bank!"

"OK OK, serious mode. Did anyone say anything about Grindr?" Bank's tone dropped.

"No, nothing. He acted normal too, so I must have blocked him quick enough."

"I never block anyone, just in case." He winked.

"Oi! You still have a Grindr profile? Does Sam know?" It was a half-joke, John knew what Bank was like.

"Having a profile doesn't mean I actually use the app."

Bank and Sam had been together nearly a year. It was the first time in the decade that he'd known John that Bank had been in what was becoming a serious relationship.

"So how are things going with Sam?"

"Good. I mean, I think good. Just sort of normal now. Not really that excited about the whole boyfriend thing anymore. You know what I mean?" He was beginning to ramble.

"Aha. The grim realities of domestic living, or are we talking blissful life and wedding bells?"

"Fuck off! I'm too young." He theatrically put his hands to his hips.

"Early thirties, that ain't too young."

"Thirties! How dare you. No way do I look in my thirties."

"Oh fuck, look who just walked in. I mean don't actually look, but for fuck's sake."

Bank half glanced. "Why? Who is she?"

"She is the biggest homophobic bitch I've ever known. Works at my school, I mean proper homophobe."

"What? In the twenty-first century these people still exist. Pathetic. I already hate her."

"She's sly too. Says the right thing in public, in school meetings, but no doubt – she hates the gays. Colleagues, students, whoever."

John accidentally looked too long in her direction and their eyes locked for a second. She acknowledged him. It looked like she tried to smile but with Allison Waugh it came out as a sort of grimace or at best a sarcastic smile.

Bank wasn't impressed. "She looks hideous. Imagine being that ugly. What is with her hair?"

Bank had a way with words and John struggled not to spit out his mouthful as he began to laugh.

"Yeah, as soon as I joined the school I was warned about her. Anyway, enough of her. You. And Sam…"

"I guess, it's great. But also, a bit dull. He's not really into partying, he likes to stay at home and watch TV. So boring. So, my friend, that is why you are coming with me to DJ Station tonight!"

"What? Not a chance!"

"Come on, like the old days. Dinner, drinks on Soi 4, drunken raunchy dancing at DJ, and I'll help you find a cute young thing to cuddle with."

"First part sounds great. Dinner, maybe a few drinks. Then I'll be relaxed at home by ten watching the football."

Bank did a mock yawn.

"Where is Sam tonight anyway?"

"Some expensive dinner with his work colleagues, then he'll meet us for a drink."

"There you go. Take him to DJ."

It was Bank's turn to laugh. "He wouldn't even go near DJ; someone might think he was gay!"

This was the real crux issue of their relationship. Sam wasn't out, and he wasn't really that interested in being out to anyone. For Bank it was becoming a major obstacle. A year and he'd never met Sam's family, who lived just outside Bangkok. Even the friends he had met didn't know Bank was Sam's partner. He was just another friend. It was starting to irritate Bank.

"Well, let's go for that drink. But we need to walk out that way, and avoid that bitch's table. I'm not even doing fake small talk with her."

TWENTY

School rumbled on, as it tended to do. Its' own repetitive journey, punctuated by a few moments that heightened students' excitement. Nutt and Danai became a kind of open secret. Most students knew they were Grade 11's hottest couple, but outside of their friendship group, few were that interested.

The football team's results had stagnated a bit, some draws left them a few points behind the top team in their attempt to win the prestigious Bangkok International School League for the first time in BSIS' history. John Jameson was pretty laid back about it, he hadn't expected them to win the championship in his first year, but the core of his team had another year at school and the potential for the following year was huge. The players wanted it badly though.

He sat in his office, alongside Miranda Scott, a rare occasion when they both had a free lesson at the same time. He talked about plans for their upcoming games against St David's and TIS – Thailand International School. They were considered the top two teams in the league, but if BSIS could beat them both they'd be champions.

"What is it with TIS? Calling themselves Thailand International School, like they represent the whole fucking nation. Arrogant assholes."

Miranda nodded in agreement. "Spot on. I hate that lot. You know the Head of PE there, Martin Buckle? Total cliché. The arrogant bullying PE teacher, gives us all a bad name."

"Yeah, ever since the first time I met him at one of those organising meetings, I took an instant dislike to him."

"I can tell you he didn't like his under-sixteen boys losing to us, with a woman coaching!"

"Twat, wait until he finds out we've got an old queen coaching the varsity boys' team!"

They both laughed, but it was true. Martin Buckle was very old school, despite only being in his thirties. He barked and made offensive comments, relentlessly.

"I think Buckle watched those Under 16s and realised how good we are going to be in the next few years."

"Yes, next year will be key. If we can combine Tee, Danai, Noom, and co. with the younger ones, bam!"

"The pressure is on John. I expect the championship next season, if not this of course! Talking of Danai, have you noticed Grade 11's cutest couple?"

John laughed. "Of course, and the kids think we don't know these things."

"I know, it's sooo cute. Nutt is punching well above his weight there too!"

They laughed at the inappropriateness of the

comment, and the fact that they both agreed. Danai was cool, popular, physically in great shape and part of the football squad. Nutt was a slightly skinny maths geek.

"Oh, for fuck's sake." John sounded genuinely irritated.

"What is it?"

"Just got an email from Walker's PA, saying he wants to see me after school about sport trips. He better not try to cancel our football trip to Phuket."

"He can't do that; the kids have already been given the information."

Jim Walker was in charge of the whole school, the principal. He preferred an off-hand approach, he was in his early sixties and close to retirement. He let Hugh Fowler deal with the day-to-day business of running the High School. He tended to stay in his office and was rarely involved with students, but just occasionally he randomly decided to stick his nose into something and interfere. Hence John's concerns about Phuket.

The trip was an annual event, hosted by the Phuket South Thailand International School. It was the biggest football event in the region, with teams from a range of countries travelling to compete in an intense four-day 7-aside competition. They usually flew down on a Wednesday evening and got back on Sunday after the finals.

He arrived at Jim's office bang on three o'clock, ready for an argument. He wasn't going to be pushed about on this.

"Hello, John. How's things? Enjoying your first year?"

"Yes, very much so. Loving the school so far."

"Super. I've heard good things John, and there is certainly a buzz about that boys' football team."

Here we go. John was sure this was Jim getting straight to the point, start with a positive comment about football. Then say the trip had to be cancelled. It was a strategy teachers used often at parents' evenings, 'the shit sandwich'. If you had something bad to say you'd make a positive comment before and after.

"Listen, I'll get straight to the point. As part of my role as principal, I am responsible for many additional things; strategic planning, child protection and safeguarding, staff behaviour, serious parental complaints, and so on."

"Yes, a vast role of course." It was a banal gap filler as John now had no idea where this conversation was going. Child protection? Was one of his students in a bad way? It was an inevitable reality of course, with hundreds of young people, some would be having a tough time. In his career he'd encountered a number of sad stories; self-harm, mental health issues, abuse. Some naïve teachers thought these things didn't happen in the world of the wealthy privately educated, but of course the reality was that money didn't stop all the complexities of adolescence and human nature.

"So, I have to investigate any issues brought to me, and I'm afraid I've received a couple of complaints about your conduct."

"What?" John was genuinely shocked. His brain began to try and process what he was hearing. Complaints about conduct?

"One relates to your behaviour outside of school, and like I said it's my duty to assess whether there is any truth to it."

"OK, Jim, I'm getting worried now. What the heck is going on?"

"I've had two colleagues speak to me in confidence about you being seen in public, shall we say, 'romantically involved' with some, well, rather young chaps."

"What? I'm sorry, Jim, what on earth is this? I hope someone is not accusing me of something."

"Goodness no, John, it's just my duty to clear up any issues, with a quiet word."

"Clear up? Issues?" He was trying to remain calm and not raise his voice, but a terrible shuddering went through his body. Had he underestimated just how evil Allison Waugh was?

"There is a part of me that wants to storm out and not even credit that with a response, but I suspect that is the reaction 'someone' wants." He made it clear that he had his suspicions about who that person was.

"Firstly, I am not romantically involved with anyone, not that it is any business of the school. Secondly, it is not really my style to be romantic in public as it happens, and thirdly I have not been dating any 'young chaps'. That clear it up?"

He exaggerated the air quotes around 'young chaps' as he very much knew what this implication meant.

"Thanks, John, I realise this is difficult, but I hope you understand I have to enquire, the school regulations don't allow me to ignore complaints. Can you think of anything that might have given someone this impression?"

"Just who are these people?"

"Obviously, I am not at liberty to say that. Any staff disclosures should remain anonymous."

"So these people can just make outlandish complaints?"

"Perhaps I've not expressed it well. I think they were genuinely more coming from the perspective of being concerned for you, about how these things could look to members of the community. To protect yourself from rumours and such like."

"I appreciate you are just the messenger here, Jim, but I do not need to protect myself. I conduct myself professionally. You do know what's really going on here, don't you?"

"Honestly, I think these comments were made in good faith."

"It's the 21st century and still we have gay men subjected to this absolute nonsense."

"I really don't think there was any homophobic element here. I mention every year to staff that we have to remember we represent the school community even outside of school. Every year I have to remind some staff about drunkenness, for example. And of course social media and all those modern issues."

"Jim, I get that this is not your fault, but I know what is going on here. There is a colleague I have been having some issues with, and I don't think the timing here is coincidental."

"Well, that is something you should discuss with your line manager, of course. I think it's also important that teachers who get on well with students need to also remember that we are teachers, not friends."

"Of course, Jim. I've been teaching quite a long

time you know."

"It's just that one of the comments, and this really is to help you, said that sometimes football training looks like you are all friends playing football. Just make sure you maintain that distance."

"Jim, I don't know who is saying this, but it's utterly absurd. I know how to coach a football squad. Team building is very important, but I am the coach, and anyone who knows anything can see that." He was trying hard not to get irate.

"Of course, of course, I'm just saying, and it's true for all of us in such a warm and friendly school, to think about the optics. I am quite sure this really is someone who is concerned for you, it wasn't a complaint per se. Just something they wanted you to be aware of."

They chatted about this and that and ended the conversation cordially. John knew it was important he remain calm in this situation.

It was clear that Jim didn't really want that hassle of this, and was just doing his job. But at the same time John didn't see old Jim Walker as someone who would understand some of the issues that gay male teachers faced at times, especially in the world of PE teaching.

He felt numb as he left the office and headed back to the PE department. He didn't know how he was meant to deal with this. It certainly wasn't something he had ever faced before.

TWENTY ONE

"So, my boy Danai advised Tee to break up with Fern. Hmm. Interesting advice buddy!" Noom gave his most devious sarcastic smile.

"Oh, come on! You think I'm that calculating?"

"Wrong question D. You should be saying, you think Tee's interested? You think Tee's jealous?

"You're crazy. Such an imagination!" Noom wasn't crazy, but Danai wasn't prepared to admit it. He had thought of little else but Tee, and Tee's single status. And Tee's smile, Tee's eyes. The way Tee looked at Danai. Or rather the way Danai hoped Tee was looking at him. It was complicated. He was now dating Nutt, but if he was honest, his feelings for Nutt were nothing compared to the yearning he had for Tee.

It had been nearly four weeks since he began dating Nutt, but Danai was starting to realise that he didn't actually know his boyfriend that well. It was different to how things were with his other friends, he was already aware that he'd never have the same close friendship with Nutt that he had with Noom, or even with Golf and the others. At times he wasn't even sure how much he actually liked Nutt, and wondered if it was just the lust and sex that he enjoyed. He seemed to like Nutt more when he was kinda on the periphery. It was weird. Is this what the early days of relationships were like? Maybe in time they'd develop the closer friendship side of things. The sex was great, two horny sixteen-year-olds exploring, sure it didn't usually last long but they tended to have the stamina to go again after a break.

Danai had spent a lot of time pondering how typical this was of him, of life. He had dreamed of having a boyfriend, his friends knowing and being chill with it. Now he had that, and he was bored. He didn't really have much in common with Nutt and he was now realising how different his boyfriend was to the nerdy perception they all had of him. No one would ever have predicted how confident and experienced Nutt seemed when they were in bed.

"So, not getting yourself a taste of Nutt tonight?"

"Is that all you think of? I'm wondering which one of us it is that you are jealous of." He said with a cheeky grin.

"Come on, it could have been worse. I could have added the word butter into that question. Anyways, where is Nutt tonight?"

"Dunno. Probably at home. Doing homework. Jerking off. I'm not his keeper!"

Noom detected a bit of an edge in his friend's voice, a slightly frustrated tone.

"OK. Just so you know you can always invite Nutt out with us. Get him more into the group. Be cool to hang out more with him, I'm sure Golf, Tee and

Beem think the same."

Tee got home from school just after four. His friends had asked him to hang out with them for a bit, but he just didn't feel like it. He'd been feeling slightly fed up of late, for reasons he didn't really understand. He'd broken up with Fern, but that was what he wanted, so he didn't get why he wasn't feeling happier.

The house was quiet. It was a Thursday so his grandparents tended to be out until just after six. His mother was almost never home before that time. She was an executive for a big marketing and media company and work inevitably took up a lot of her time and energy. Tee and his mum had lived with his mum's parents since his dad had tragically died when Tee was still a toddler. Initially the plan had been to move in with the grandparents for a short time, to help with the childcare. The arrangement worked well and they decided to make it permanent. Tee's grandparents owned one of those big old houses close to school and not far from the river. It would have been worth a fortune if they'd wanted to sell. They didn't. The house had been in the family for generations. On paper the family was rich, by virtue of that house, but they never had much spare cash. Tee's mum had a good salary and the money she had inherited from her husband when he died had been put in a fund to pay for Tee's expensive education. Tee had never thought of his family as being rich, although of course they were, compared to most. But, some of Tee's friends were proper hi-so rich – expensive European holidays, fancy cars and all sorts.

He dumped his school bag in the corner of his

room, he did have some homework but he'd get to it later. He lay on his bed and idly flicked through his phone.

He thought again about his break up with Fern, he knew it had been coming. The more she had wanted their relationship to become more physical, the more he knew it was going to have to end. He just didn't want to have sex with her, and he didn't really know why. Perhaps he should chat more with Beem, he felt they had bonded more after their night-out chat. Golf had kept making those jokes about how infrequently Beem jerked off. Tee had just laughed and acted super mature, classic Tee-style, but the truth was that from what he could work out he probably jerked off even less than Beem. He was sure something must be wrong with him. He was meant to have raging hormones, and a crazy high sex-drive. He was a seventeen-year-old boy for fuck's sake. Sometimes Noom would talk about jerking off two or three times a day, and he wasn't joking.

For Tee, once every two weeks was the absolute max. In bed, in the dark. He'd grab a wad of tissue from his bedside table and fully cover his dick, to make sure there was no extra mess at all. He did have quite a few wet dreams, but his google research had told him that was normal, and probably a result of his infrequent jerking. He hated waking up to that sticky mess, on his sheets and boxers.

The idea of Fern touching his dick kinda repulsed him. He didn't want someone else doing that. The only thing they had ever done was hug, a little. She had kissed him a few times, but one time when she tried to use her tongue he had jolted back in horror. So they had to break up. He had no choice. The last thing he wanted was for a frustrated Fern to start spreading rumours around about Tee's sexual problems. He had been reading up about being asexual and wondered if that was what he was. He wasn't sure though. It didn't seem to quite fit.

He saw someone had posted a picture of him on Instagram, playing football. The caption was 'BSIS. Captain. Legend.' He did quite enjoy his superstar status at school, he couldn't deny that. He wasn't an arrogant person but he did like how people looked up to him, even teachers. He was always treated as the leader. He loved his little friendship group, with its mix of personalities, each one having their role in the clique. He was enjoying his developing friendship with Danai too, they had grown much closer now in Grade 11. He loved how Danai was quite open in telling Tee things. He was a little bit jealous of Nutt and Danai, he had never had that relaxed confidence with Fern. How cool was it to be such a self-assured couple in Grade 11? Even more so since they were both guys, and here he was breaking up with apparently the hottest girl in school!

His mum texted.

Don't eat early. I'll be home by six we can go for steak. Le Château.

Wow! Awesome!

They both loved Le Château, a homely little local French restaurant. The owners were a long-time French expat and his Thai wife, their children had also studied at BSIS but were now at university in Europe. Tee always appreciated how much his mum tried to make time even in her busy work life.

Nan and Gramps coming?

What do you think?

He replied with a laughing sticker. His grandparents almost never came out with them. Unless it was a special occasion or a place that was really good value. 'I can cook steak at home', was a typical response from his grandmother. They also never liked to eat much later than six. Their Thursday routine was to go to the nearby supermarket and eat in the cheap food court there. That was their weekly treat, spending about fifty baht on simple chicken and rice. The rest of the week his grandmother would cook, and they'd be in bed early. They were approaching seventy. Ancient as far as Tee was concerned.

TWENTY TWO

John Jameson had been completely thrown by his meeting with Jim Walker. He had been warned about Allison, and of course he had already noticed her homophobia, but this level of evil was not something he could ever have seen coming. Her particular brand of homophobia was quite nuanced, and the sort that only a gay man was likely to quickly detect. She played the role of trying to look like a modern liberal educator. However, there were so many inconsistencies that her snarling bullying personality was never that far from the surface.

John was determined that he would not act any differently after these preposterous complaints had been made. He had always had a great rapport with students, that was what made him good at his job. That's why he stood out from many of his colleagues, he showed students respect, talked to them like people, and listened. The nature of teaching, in a country like Thailand meant you could have a more relaxed vibe in the classroom, and engage in some friendly banter. Behaviour was never really an issue. But he always maintained a professional core.

He walked through the study lounge, on his way to his office.

"Yo! Mr Jameson! How's tricks?" Noom shouted across the room.

"How's tricks?" John spoke with mock disapproval. "Very good, thanks, Noom, how are you?"

"I'm awesome. Ready for the big game? We'll thrash them. My boy Danai will run riot." Noom put his arm affectionately around Danai as he spoke.

John had tried very hard to be completely natural around Danai, since the Grindr event. He was always looking for signs though. Was Danai behaving differently around him? Was he quieter? Awkward?

"Confidence is great, boys, but be careful of overconfidence."

"Dude, I mean, coach, come on! We are on fire. This boy's like the Thai Messi." He gave his buddy a pat on the cheek. Danai pushed him away "he's crazy".

Miss Waugh appeared at the door to her office. "Can you please keep that noise down? Oh, Mr Jameson, I didn't realise it was you."

As if. The passive aggressive bitch knew exactly who was out there talking.

"Many apologies, Miss Waugh. Football match excitement. I am sure you are aware of the big game tomorrow." He turned back to the students "Boys, will you ask Tee to come and see me when he's in? Need a chat with the captain before I confirm the team."

Allison Waugh skulked back into her office with

another disapproving glare.

As soon as their coach was out of earshot and on the way to his office, the boys began to theorise.

"You think he knows?"

"Knows what? That you stalked him on Grindr?"

"Fuck off!"

"Chill, D. He doesn't know. He was totally normal."

"What's with her though? It's before school and she's already complaining."

"She's got issues. Issue with me, hates men. For sure. Have you ever seen her tell the girls to be quiet with their noisy gossiping?"

Nutt arrived a few minutes later, there were still only a handful of people in the common room area. He squeezed Danai's shoulder and gave him a quick peck on the cheek.

"Morning, babe."

Danai smiled. It sounded good, even if he was a little unsure about the relationship.

Noom showed his disapproval, pretending to vomit "Get a room!"

"Oh, that's an idea!" The boys laughed.

Waugh seemed to scowl again from her office desk.

"Shit. Did she see you kiss me?"

"Kiss? Call that a kiss. I'll show her a kiss."

Nutt leaned in before Danai jokingly slapped his face.

"That would wind her up too much. No one's kissed her for decades; you can be sure of that."

"Wanna come back to my place after school?" Nutt had a cheeky grin and winked.

Danai shyly nodded. "Cool."

"Enough already! We get it, you guys are Grade 11's hottest item! And you can't take my boy every day. Danoom must live on!"

"You jealous, Noom?"

"Yeah, you damn right I am, but not of either of you. Just of you both getting some. Fuck, man, I need some of that."

"Always gotta bring it down to your level…"

"Oh, D baby, you'd love to get down to my level!" Noom laughed as if his joke was both the most original and most amusing ever.

The common room filled with the usual hustle and bustle of the early morning. Tee walked in slowly.

"Tee, Jamo wants you, buddy," Danai shouted and noticed Miss Waugh raise her head again.

"What?"

"Not another one who wants him!" Noom again laughed at his own joke.

"To speak about the game or something, high-level confidential tactics stuff, in his office."

Tee dropped his bag by his friends and trudged towards the PE department office. He tapped on the door and walked in.

"Morning, Tee. How you doing?"

"Danai said you wanted to see me?" Tee sounded unusually subdued.

"Yes, yes. The game. Any thoughts about team selection? How are the boys feeling?"

John felt the coach-captain relationship was important, even in school football. Tee played a key role, not just on the pitch, but in keeping up the camaraderie and spirit in the squad.

"Pretty usual, Mr J, we'll be OK."

They spoke briefly about tactics. John felt it was

key to keep it tight in midfield and not shy away from any tough tackling.

"They've got skilful players Tee, but so have we, and we are better at the physical side of the game."

"Yeah, I guess."

"Everything OK, Tee?

"Just one of those days."

"Well, if you need to talk you know you can pop over here any time."

"Thanks. Just life, you know."

"Sounds pretty heavy. Anything specifically getting you down?"

Tee paused, and sighed. "I broke up with Fern."

"Oh, I'm sorry to hear that. Yes, that's always going to be rough."

"No, I mean it's fine. I wanted to break up. It's just weird. I can't really explain."

It wasn't an unusual story for a teacher to hear. School relationships tended to be fickle, but John had realised that Tee had a maturity beyond his seventeen years. He was just the sort to start dating at school and be with that person forever. Evidently not. It was clear that he was deeply affected over his break up but John knew not to press him to talk about it. He'd always been one of those teachers that students knew they could confide in, or ask advice. The key reason for that was that students felt comfortable with him and knew they could speak to him openly, without judgement. He didn't push things. Let students speak if they want to, was always his motto. He had seen many a young teacher try too hard to be the cool teacher students could speak to. They'd put students off by over-playing the 'you can talk to me' thing. Teenagers were very capable of sussing out which teachers could be a good ear, and which couldn't.

"Well, as you say, Tee, life. Ups and downs eh? Keep yourself busy is always top advice. So the match can help, and so can your friends of course."

"Yes. So what's your thinking coach? Same team?"

"I've been thinking it's time to give Sun a start in midfield."

Sun was probably the least naturally skilful player in the squad, but he was also perhaps the strongest, and he had an infamously short fuse. His chances had been slightly limited as he was frequently sent off in the under-sixteen team. In one match he threw a punch that resulted in a school suspension and the organising committee banning him from playing in their knockout tournament. For John Jameson he was something of a risk. Playing with a man down in a 7-a-side was near on impossible.

"Oh, I like your thinking, unleash the Korean! Risky though." Tee smiled.

Students always talked about Sun as Korean, even though his dad was Thai. His mum was Korean though and it gave him that exotic air. Korea had replaced Japan as the height of cool and Sun liked to embrace his Korean heritage.

"Risky indeed Tee. So it's the captain's job to get him in the zone. I want him angry, snarling, and hard-tackling but staying the right side of that line between physicality and violence!"

"Got ya, coach. Leave it with me. Can I tell him he is playing?"

"Yep, I will put the team up soon anyway. Big him up, this is his moment to show his worth to the team."

Tee walked out with more of a purposeful stride.

He loved these meetings with Mr Jameson, it made him feel important and trusted, and he loved how seriously Mr Jameson took school sport.

TWENTY THREE

The boys always found it difficult to focus on the day of a big match, and much to the annoyance of Miss Waugh, the head of school agreed with John that the squad could leave their last lesson thirty minutes early. To give them extra time to change, warm up, and get ready for the big game.

When the game began there was a raucous atmosphere. It felt like most students had stayed behind to watch the contest. A win would give BSIS a shot at the league title with their final game away at the top team, TIS. The game went beautifully and exactly according to plan. Sun was fired up and tackling hard, but fair. Tee had taken him to one side put an arm around him and basically told him he was the most important player on the pitch. Sun was determined and motivated. He was warned once by the ref after committing a succession of minor fouls, but overall the tactic worked perfectly. Minutes before half-time the St David's midfielder was slow to a tackle, scared off by Sun's physicality. Sun was able to run at the defence slip a perfect pass to Danai who was able to use his pace to beat the defender and hammer the ball into the back of the net. The crowd erupted, as did the players, piling on Danai in celebration. Tee made sure to give Sun the credit too.

Coach Jameson was typically serious, angrily shouting at his team to stop the celebrations and keep their heads in the game. His half-time team talk had the perfect blend of praise, and keeping them on edge with the usual 'only halfway', 'job not done' clichés.

He gave Sun a hearty pat on the back. "If I was one to swear I'd say, 'Sun, you effing beauty.' Bloody brilliant, get a drink and rest up. I'll switch Tom in for you and bring you back just when St David's think you've gone for the day!"

Sun had no complaints. He was exhausted after thirty minutes of hard running and knew he was probably close to a yellow card.

The second half was a tense affair, BSIS were really entering the big time now, against one of the top teams, and winning. Jameson was nervous on the touchline, desperately wanting that second goal to give them some breathing space. Tee was expertly controlling things at the back, barking orders and leading counterattacks. Elegantly driving forward out of defence and picking out killer passes. They couldn't find that goal though.

Danai was having a quiet second half and he was disappointed when the coach subbed him off.

"Take some liquids on Danai, and keep yourself warmed up for a final burst of energy."

"Sure, coach."

Nutt smiled at him, Danai gave a half wave but was too focused on the match and in that competitive zone.

It was invariably the way with their games that aside from the goalkeeper only Tee would play the full hour. He had strength and stamina way beyond the levels of the rest of the squad and his importance to the team was too great. He would generally only get a break when the boys were winning easily.

Danai was brought back on for the final five minutes and the tactic worked perfectly, with St David's tiring and frustrated by their inability to create any clear chances to equalise, the pacey winger latched onto a long ball then ran at the defence again and expertly finished in the bottom corner.

The school erupted. Teachers cheering, students jumping up and down and hugging each other.

John tried to remain cool and calm with a clenched fist before shouting his trademark 'keep the focus boys'.

Danai was mobbed by his teammates. Tee gave him a football celebration style kiss on his forehead and roared. It sent shivers throughout Danai's body. He knew it was just a football celebration, but he also loved how Tee was the most tactile on the team.

At the final whistle the boys surrounded Coach Jameson, with hearty pats on the back and slightly over-the-top attempts to hug him, such was the atmosphere. Once it had all calmed down he was straight back to the serious business.

"Good win, boys, but TIS will be a much tougher game, we need more of the same again, but we have to be more ruthless. We left it very late here to get that breathing space."

He wouldn't normally have put a dampener on such a good display but he had been worried about over confidence creeping in and the atmosphere at the end confirmed it. The players seemed to think winning the league was inevitable.

Tee immediately chipped in, "Agree, coach, we should have been two or three goals up in the first half, and we nearly let them back in the game. That was harder work than it should have been."

Tee was acutely away of his job and at times like this it was important he reiterated what the coach said, even if he didn't fully agree. Tee and Coach Jameson were the two most respected members of the squad. If they both thought the same, everyone took note.

"OK, you two, agreed, but… what about those two beauties from my boy Danai!" Noom screamed it from the top of his lungs to huge cheers from the players. "He's not just the sexiest school football player in town!"

Danai rolled his eyes as the squad laughed.

Allison Waugh who had been watching from the balcony shuffled back in to her office.

"Whaaat? Did *she* actually watch a game?" Danai didn't care that the scorn in his voice was obvious.

"I doubt she watched. Maybe she came out at the end to complain about the noise." John gave a sly grin as the boys cheered again.

"Coach Jameson, you know the best thing about a game on a Friday?"

"No, what is it Noom?"

"We can go out tonight and get the beers in! You gonna join us?" More cheers.

"Number one. No I will not be joining your night out. Number two, you are obviously joking about beer as you are all underage and I'd have to report any law breaking. So, very amusing."

"Of course we are joking, aren't we, boys?" Noom said in his best sarcastic voice.

Eventually, the euphoria dissipated and fans and players headed home. Of course John knew the players *would* party in the way stated. They also knew that it was important that John officially 'didn't know'. School could be a complicated business at times, when to turn a blind eye was one of the biggest judgement calls a teacher had to make. John usually made them well.

John strolled back through the sixth form centre to his office. He was buzzing. He had contained his excitement in front of the players but he was fired up. As he walked by her office Allison barked out to him "I take it from all that noise that it was a good result or something?"

"Indeed it was, 2-0 win. Oh, so you didn't get to see the game?"

"Football's not really my thing?" She said in her typically caustic manner.

She just didn't get it. Her job here was to support these very students, that's what watching school sport was all about. Whether you enjoyed the sporting spectacle itself was irrelevant. The school Maths department were notoriously clueless about sport, but they were all there cheering on their students.

"Well, they all seemed very over-excited." She let the statement hang there. It was typically passive aggressive. She was exhausting, but John was in too good a mood to let her wind him up.

"And rightly so, that's a great achievement for BSIS. These boys are putting the school on the map, we now have a chance of winning the league championship."

"Err, shouldn't school sport be about more than just winning," she bit back.

"Indeed, and it *is* about more than winning. We play for health, for fun, for camaraderie, for increased self-esteem, and guess what? With players like that we also play to win and compete!"

She smiled in her patronising way. Even her smile was nasty.

"What a shame that a woman of your age has never learnt the multi-faceted benefits of sport. Anyway, have a nice weekend. Do some exercise and try not to work too late, it's Friday." He was already ten metres away from her door before she even had the chance to reply.

TWENTY FOUR

Tee took his role as captain, very seriously. He insisted that all the squad joined on the evening celebration. It was an important aspect of being part of the squad, in his opinion. They'd go to a typical open-air bar and restaurant fairly close to school. The food was great and it wasn't the sort of place they would ask for ID from a few young footballers celebrating a win with a couple of cold beers. He knew that only about half the squad would be keen for the evening to continue at a trendier bar or club in town. He certainly wasn't going to make *that* part of the evening compulsory. The likes of Sun, despite his bad-boy persona on the pitch, was not a partier. He would rarely stay out beyond ten o'clock on these nights.

Danai walked home with Nutt and Noom, to shower and change before the night out.

"It's so unfair that it's squad members only. I wanna celebrate with my hot boyfriend," Nutt complained.

"Well, you've got over an hour until we go out. That's enough time to celebrate… more than once." Noom roared with laughter in his usual style.

"Oh, p-lease! Always so predictably crude." Danai shook his head.

Noom winked at his best mate. "And you love it!" As soon as Noom had turned right towards his place, and arranged to meet at their usual spot (outside 7-Eleven), Nutt whispered "Yeah, I wanna celebrate with my hands all over your sweaty body."

"Eww." Danai wasn't sure what to make of that.

"You smell so manly. It's so fucking hot."

Danai changed the subject. "Are you really annoyed about not coming tonight?"

"No, of course not. You know I don't really get that whole football banter. I just want to spend time with you."

They walked in the door to Danai's house. His parents weren't home from work yet. As soon as Nutt established this he dropped to his knees and pulled down Danai's football shorts.

"Nice underwear."

"Nutt, I should shower first."

"No! Let's get dirtier first, then shower. Your dick doesn't seem like it wants me to stop touching it."

It was true. Like most seventeen-year-old boys, Danai had little control over it. He was instantly rock-hard, even before Nutt had released it from the tight briefs. Nutt was frantically sucking, eyes closed, both in ecstasy.

"Fuck that feels amazing. Don't stop." Nutt had no intention of stopping. He loved the sweatiness, the sweaty smell, and the sleaziness of going down on his boyfriend as soon as they were in the house.

Occasionally, Nutt paused to draw breath or to tease his lover with a flick of his tongue. Danai was so lost in the moment that he practically forced his dick back into Nutt's mouth. It turned Nutt on so much that his sweet, shy boyfriend was acting in this dominant way.

"Fuck. Fuck." Danai's grasp of vocabulary had become rather more basic in the height of passion. Nutt groaned; it was such an intense horny moment.

"Fuck, I'm gonna cum."

Nutt put both his hands on Danai's ass cheeks to hold him closer.

"Nutt, I'm gonna cum…" The grip with which Nutt was holding him made it clear to Danai what his lover wanted. Danai instinctively put both hands on Nutt's head as he finished. He continued to hold Nutt's head as his body jerked.

"Fuck. Oh, my god. Fuck that was good. I can't believe you swallowed all that."

Danai began to giggle as Nutt stood up and lent in to kiss him.

Danai backed away. "Ewww, no way."

"It's your cum, babe."

"Right, I need to shower. Don't have much time now."

The slightly shy boyfriend had returned. They went upstairs, Nutt lying on the bed looking through Instagram while Danai showered.

They regularly started an evening at Isan Garden, it hit all the key things. Good food, relaxed atmosphere, cheap beer, and the owner Ae and her husband took a very relaxed view to the enforcing of Thailand's drinking laws. The boys never got drunk there, they'd just order a few beers with food, and they were regular customers who always tipped well. Miss Ae was very happy to have their custom. Tee had actually been in the day before to book a table for fifteen people. He didn't tell the squad this as they would think he was tempting fate. He justified it by thinking to himself they were due a squad night out, win, lose, or draw.

Ae had known Tee since he was twelve or thirteen. He had always been a polite and sensible boy. Occasionally he'd eat there with his family. It was that sort of place. Despite the plastic tables and cheap vibe, the food was so good that it attracted people from all walks of life. The location, close to Bangkok's busy business district meant they got a lot of the after-work crowd who wanted food and drinks before heading to one of Silom's nightspots.

The entire squad were on time, not necessarily a normal occurrence, but they took football seriously and they considered this a football event. Tee gave a short speech, along the lines that they'd done so well but now it was serious. Just one more win and they'd be league champions for the first time in the history of BSIS. 'Just one more win' was something of an understatement. TIS has been the top school team in the city for years, and been consistently good for decades. BSIS were very much the upstarts. Tee told the squad they were strictly not to order beers, yet. They complained, but quickly realised why. Coach Jameson strolled into the restaurant to a huge roar from the squad.

"Jamoooo!" Some of the players screamed.

"I'm not staying, boys, just wanted to pop in and

show my face. Well done today, top stuff. Don't be out too late, and I am pleased to see no one breaking the law with any alcohol."

He chatted and stayed for five minutes, despite Noom's best efforts to persuade him to stay. He had been more than happy to oblige when Tee asked if he could just drop in to say hello. He knew from a lifetime of playing team sports, just how important that team ethic was. Tee walked him to the entrance and thanked him for coming.

"No problem, Tee, I take this as seriously as you guys do. Don't let them get out of control!"

As soon as Tee sat back down, Noom took over "Cold beers all round!" The squad cheered in agreement.

Even Sun cheered, despite the fact that he'd only drink a few small glasses. As predicted, half of the squad headed home after the meal. The rest planned to head up to Khao San Road where they'd meet up with Nutt, Beem and whoever else might be about. Non-football players were free to join for that part of the evening.

TWENTY FIVE

Bangkok's football schedule meant the league season was always over by Christmas. The big event in the New Year was the tournament down on Phuket Island. It lasted four days and attracted teams from all over Asia. Competition was intense, they'd be a group stage over the first two days, and then eight teams qualified for the knockout stages. Saturday would be the quarters and semis with the final on Sunday morning.

John Jameson and Miranda Scott had planned it very carefully. They'd be taking four teams this year. The Under 16s and Under 19s in both boys and girls categories. It wasn't a guarantee which teams they'd take, and with the intensity of the event they knew they could only take teams that were good enough to compete.

The second time John was summoned to a meeting with Principal Walker, it really was about the Phuket tournament.

"Hi, John, good to see you. Now straight to

business. We've been discussing the football tournament in leadership meetings."

"Great to hear that interest in our teams is growing." John tried to sound relaxed.

"Of course, now obviously you and Miranda will lead the teams, but I think we should adjust the other staffing."

"Right, OK. No problem. Any reason why?"

"Well just we don't want to impact too heavily on other departments, all sorts of complexities."

John was open to any suggestions. He was suspicious though. The four staff who had been due to go were all friends, and he was sure Allison Waugh was behind this, wanting to cause trouble. No doubt she had found out that Tom Stevens, who was coaching the Under 16 squad, was also gay and she didn't think two gay men should be on the same trip. That was the sort of attitude she'd have.

"No problem, Jim, what do you suggest?"

"I think that Tom Stevens should probably stay in Bangkok, we don't want his classes missing too many important lessons."

"OK, that would be a shame as Tom has worked hard with the Under 16 squad, but we will work it out."

"Thanks John, I am sure you can. I thought that Matt Jones would be a good alternative."

John was actually pretty happy with the suggestion. He chuckled inside. Perhaps Allison had misread Matt Jones. He was dour and quiet and had a stern reputation. He was certainly quite a traditional family man, who went to church on occasions, but John had got on well with him and he knew that Matt liked his football.

John played his hand well. "Well I don't know Matt well, but I am sure he will be perfect if he is happy to go."

During the following week, the only thing the boys could think about was the championship-deciding match with TIS. They were two points behind, so the equation was simple. They had to win to clinch the championship, anything else would mean TIS would be able to swagger in the glory of yet another victorious season. John Jameson tried to keep the team relaxed, frequently saying that whatever the result it would be good preparation for the Phuket tournament. He also made it clear that he felt they were a year ahead of schedule. It was the following season he expected them to challenge for the championship.

It was true that the Phuket tournament was the most prestigious event in school football in the region, and there would be four or five schools there who were better than TIS. Some of the big schools from Hong Kong and Malaysia always had very strong teams.

John's focus was on getting that balance right, and making sure he managed their expectations. They had done so well, and confidence was sky high, but he knew TIS were technically a stronger team, and much more experienced. It would be hard to beat them. Especially as the game was played at the TIS school campus. Their impressive campus was intimidating, twice as large as BSIS and much slicker and modern. They had a superb football pitch surrounded by bleachers which always resulted in a big crowd of their students cheering them on.

Danai lay back on his bed, flicking through his phone while keeping up to date with the Line group for the football squad, as well as his individual chats with Noom, Nutt and whoever else.

Tee's messages to the group were typically sensible and mature.

Don't overdo it this week. Rest. Eat healthy.

Tee then sent Danai a private message. It always caused a little shudder of excitement.

So don't tire yourself out with Nutt! ;)

Danai sent back a shocked face sticker.

He was shocked, kinda. Tee talking to him about sex. He wanted to reply, 'I'd love to tire myself out with you!'

He sent Tee a selfie.

See, just me here, no Nutt!

Tee followed with his own. He was topless. A quickly taken selfie that looked so good it could have been a carefully posed professional model shot.

Danai squealed with lust. What was Tee doing to him?

How the fuck do you always look so good?

Ha-Ha. Are you flirting with me, Danai?

In my dreams! You are way out of my league!

Danai quickly followed with a laughing sticker, just so Tee knew he was 'joking'.

Come on, Danai, we are in the same league. For sure. Both hotties!

They both followed with laughter. But for Danai this was laughter tinged with pain, Tee calling him a hottie, in jest.

Danai sent a screenshot of the chat to Noom.

Is Tee flirting with me? WTAF!

Fuck, my boy Danai got it bad!

No, no. I'm over Tee now. I'm with Nutt, remember!

He lied. He knew he lied. He knew that Noom knew he was lying.

Danai, Danai, Danai. You can't fool me. Come on!

Talking of Nutt, he just texted. He is on the way over. Gotta shower.

Fuck you! I gotta jerk again.

Danai ended the conversation with a shy sticker, then a vomiting one.

When Nutt arrived they went straight up the stairs to Danai's room.

"Tee told the squad not to get too much exercise!"

"OK, baby, message received. You lay back on the bed and let me look after my man."

Danai got naked and did exactly that. He had a wave of guilt, that he was being a selfish lover, he just didn't feel like sucking Nutt and he preferred it like this. Sometimes when he closed his eyes he tried to imagine he was with Tee, it was awesome, but of course he then felt more guilty, after the act.

Danai didn't last long. He was getting better at controlling himself, but at seventeen his hormones were such that he often finished quickly.

Nutt's skill and noises didn't help. Danai had moaned "I'm close, baby" in the hope that Nutt would rest his mouth and tongue, he didn't. He sped up.

"Fuck that was so fucking good."

"You taste good too, what you eating today?"

Danai blushed, it still weirded him out, this was not something he wanted to do to Nutt, but Nutt seemed to genuinely love it.

"Dunno, maybe all the pineapple I snacked on earlier?"

"Yeah, soooo sweet."

"Sorry I'm so, err fast. We should try and make it last longer next time."

"Sure, baby."

Nutt didn't stay too long. Danai said he needed to sleep well all week because of the football match. Nutt almost rolled his eyes; he just didn't get the whole football obsession.

He texted Noom again.

Oh, I see, Nutt gone has he? Now you talk to

me again.

Yeah. Lols.

OMG! A quick booty call. Fuck you are so annoying. It's so unfair.

They chatted about this and that and nothing much.

The day of the big game arrived. John Jameson had sent an email to all staff to say the squad would miss the last two lessons of the day, after lunch. He wanted to make sure they took no risks on the traffic and that they'd be there in plenty of time to warm up before the 3.30pm kick-off.

Allison Waugh screeched as John walked past her office. "Err Mr Jameson, can I have a word?" It was a high pitch squeal that for some had the same effect as fingernails down a blackboard.

"Sure Allison, how can I help?"

"I'm sorry but I thought football matches are meant to be after school."

"Yes they are, but there can be a lot of afternoon traffic and TIS is the furthest match we have to travel to."

"Well, I am not happy about it. I think you need to call them and have the game put back later."

"I see. I'm not sure that's possible. Fortunately, you not being happy doesn't have a bearing on the Bangkok International School's Football League. God help us all if it did."

"Excuse me. I do not like your attitude. The students should not be missing curriculum time. I think you have forgotten what we are here for."

"Allison, I am not wasting my time having the conversation with you. It's important to the school. In fact, Jim and Hugh will be travelling with us to the game. Frankly it's shocking, but not surprising, that you don't support students here, at all."

He stormed out. Furious. She was something else.

He was relieved when the whole squad were safely on the team bus. He had been nervous, half expecting an email from Hugh Fowler saying he had contacted TIS to delay kick-off a bit. Perhaps Allison realised she wasn't going to win this one, so just contented herself with having her moan. He had subtly enquired of Hugh, who simply replied "I've been so busy getting things done before this game John, I've barely even had time to check e-mails." He grinned.

John sat down with a smug satisfaction. He had already told the boys the team. Again, Sun was given a starting role in a defensive capacity. He was to stick to their star man like glue. 'Don't give him space and DO NOT allow shots from the edge of the box' was the message.

Tam Puttawattana was a Thai national youth player and the outstanding talent in the TIS team. When BSIS played TIS in the younger age range a year or so earlier they had done well, kept it tight, but Tam had scored three times in the second half, all brilliant goals. The 4-1 final score seemed like a thrashing.

Some of the boys weren't sure of John's defensive strategy, but they would go with it. They trusted his judgement. He was clear that the first fifteen minutes were crucial. 'Don't give them the confidence of an early goal, that's all that matters.' He didn't care if they had any opportunities themselves in the early part of the game. He had told Danai to operate with caution. The key was making sure the opposition knew there were in a game.

He had seen plenty of TIS over the years and early goals were their lethal weapon. They'd score in the first four or five minutes and quickly demoralise teams, adding more goals at will. He was convinced if they could hold it tight then they whole complexion would change.

They were lucky with traffic and they arrived very early. He cheekily smiled at Hugh "Well, we could have left later perhaps!"

Tee organised the boys with a gentle warm up on the pitch and some shooting practice.

Some of the other students actually arrived just before kick-off, which ended up being nearer 3.45pm. He wondered if Allison would find out that technically they could have left at the end of the day. Part of him hoped so, just to wind her up. But he could do without the hassle.

The start of the game was tense, TIS started brightly and had one or two decent chances. Sun was doing his job well though, depriving Tam of any space on the ball.

John made the first change after twenty minutes; they boys were starting to get frustrated at the defensive approach and he felt the message had got through to TIS. This was a serious game. He took Sun off and replaced him with Nik, who had more attacking flair.

"Bloody brilliant, Sunny, get a drink and keep those muscles loose, you will be back on."

The positive start turned to delirium just before

half-time, a nice patch of passing between Nik and Danai resulted in Tee smashing home from the edge of the box.

The players went crazy, John frantically and almost angrily telling them to calm down. He was excited inside and felt it was a nice little win from a coach's tactical perspective. He had got his strategy spot on and the team were a goal up at half-time. Tam Puttawattana angrily kicked a water bottle as they took their half-time team talk.

"Focus. Too much over-excitement at the end there, you almost lost this lead immediately. This game is going to get much harder, you ain't seen nothing yet." John was worked up, and slightly annoyed. The players had almost criminally let the lead go immediately, losing concentration in their celebrations and relying on a great save from Sam in goal and another brilliant tackle from Tee, all in the last two minutes of the half.

"Now keep hydrated and get the heads in place. Sun quick warm up, you are starting the second half. Danai, take a break." He nodded to Tee to take over. They were a well-oiled double act.

Danai was gutted, but knew it made good sense, he was feeling exhausted from the all the running he had done.

The second half started in similar fashion to the first, BSIS trying to hold it firm, but this time TIS finally found a way through. There was nothing the boys could do about it, a moment of brilliance from Tam and one of his teammates had a simple tap-in to equalise.

The last ten minutes were frantic, Danai back on as BSIS tried to force a winning goal. John was trying to keep everyone calm from the sidelines, but the boys were in panic mode and lost their calm focus, and with it their quality began to desert them.

John was particularly annoyed with the TIS coach, Martin Buckle, an arrogant Brit who kept barking out "That's it boys we've got them beat here, they are rattled, let's just see it out." There was no call for that in John's mind. Of course there was some truth in what he was saying, but it was poor sportsmanship, nonetheless.

With a minute to go Danai had a flash shot that hit the outside of the post and with it the team's chance of their first ever championship had slipped by. When the referee blew the final whistle they were devastated. Yes, they had had a great season and the draw with TIS showed the progress that had been made, but it was hard to be thinking rationally in the moment. They had come so close.

John said all the right clichés. "Top performance, boys, just that bit of luck that eluded us. We'll get them next time. Make no mistake, the balance of power in Bangkok football is shifting our way."

Danai's shoulders slumped as he traipsed off. "I should have scored."

"You were awesome, D, and that was a great fucking effort." Tee put his arm warmly around his friend and squeezed his shoulder, affectionately. In the drama of the match and with such disappointment Danai didn't really take stock of him walking off with Tee's embrace.

Martin Buckle was as annoying as ever. To John he was a big thug, he did some Thai boxing and was the stereotype of all that was wrong about Brits in Bangkok. He drank heavily and it was an open secret that he regularly cheated on his wife with women he picked up from Bangkok's seediest bars.

"Well done, John lad, you boys made us work for it. Not a bad little team you've got there."

John smiled through gritted teeth "Thanks, Martin. Well played."

"Right, better get these boys ready for another trophy celebration. It almost gets boring!"

John made sure the boys did a slight warm-down and were hydrated. He kept his post-match talk to a minimum, he didn't need to say much.

"Remember this moment, boys, it will make our future victories all the sweeter. We don't want to feel this again."

The bus journey back to school wasn't too sombre, the boys focused on the irritating TIS coach or some of their players whosc swagger annoyed them. John liked what he was hearing, they were already motivating themselves to succeed in the future.

TWENTY SIX

The next day at school Hugh Fowler gave a nice shoutout to the team in assembly, words about how proud they'd done the school and such.

Allison Waugh was less pleasant when John passed her later in the day. She called him into her office for a chat. "After all that fuss, they lost? Oh dear."

"It was a draw, Allison."

"Well, it's done now. I need to take a closer look at the time taken in this school for football."

"For goodness sake, Allison, let it go. You must have better things to do in your role here, surely?"

"Looking after the well-being of students is exactly my role. This whole football obsession has an unhealthy feel to it."

She was as bitter as ever, but there was a sinister edge to her.

"You need to accept that sport is a key part of school."

"I don't have a problem with sport, it's your attitude that's the issue. I don't like your relationship with the students. You need to be very careful."

"What are you talking about?" John didn't like where this was going, but it at least confirmed his worst suspicions.

"You are not here to try and promote your lifestyle Mr Jameson. I will repeat, you need to be very careful. You wouldn't want rumours to start spreading that could damage your career. Even a false rumour would be career-ending."

"Are you threatening me?"

"I am just observing you with students and giving you some friendly advice. You wouldn't want people to get the wrong idea."

"Right, I am terminating this meeting. Do not call me in to your office again without another member of staff present."

She smiled, her most vile of smiles. "Seems I may have hit a nerve."

He walked out, seething. He was almost shaking with anger. He had to sit down and get some calm time to consider how on earth he should approach this horror. Not for the first time he felt he may have underestimated just how evil Allison Waugh was. She was clearly now threatening to start spreading malicious rumours. 'Lifestyle'. That was a classic euphemistic bit of homophobia. This was not what he expected in 21st century Thailand.

The last week of term was typically euphoric, lots of celebratory events at school. The first semester was always such a long one that there was a strong sense of relief for both teachers and students when it finally reached a conclusion.

For the football squad there was a fun match

against teachers, or teachers plus Tee. The teachers were one player short so to balance the numbers they took one of the students. There was a mixture of laughs and jeers from the squad when Miranda Scott announced that they had "randomly picked one player, Tee."

Apart from the PE department the rest of the staff team tended to be men in their thirties whose best football days were long past. John, Miranda, and Tee kept the staff team in the match, but only just. They ended up losing an entertaining match 6-3, with Danai bagging a brilliant hat-trick. There was something of a party atmosphere with teachers and students cheering loudly.

The most notable moment, at least from Danai's perspective, came just towards the end. He was challenging for a loose ball with Tee, the result of which led to both players tumbling to the turf. Tee effectively landed right on top of Danai, a position Danai had often daydreamed about. Tee giggled as he lay on Danai and their eyes locked. It was a fleeting moment, probably not much more than a second but in that moment Danai was sure that Tee was going to lower his head and kiss him passionately. It was as if there was no one else around, and they were alone in the moment. Danai was sure he had closed his eyes in anticipation. Tee gently slapped Danai's face and got up laughing.

"I love ya, buddy, but you ain't winning the ball off me!"

Danai looked around, surprised to see everyone acting normally. No one seemed to have noticed his special moment. He assumed it was just his imagination running wild, until Noom texted him late that evening.

WTF! I thought Tee was gonna kiss you.

Yes! You noticed? It really felt like that.

Yeah. I'm starting to think there may be something in your fantasy.

Don't tease me with hope!

Anyway, you got Nutt now, lots of Nutt.

Lame, Noom!

They signed off. It had been a great semester for Danai. He had a boyfriend, even if he wasn't totally sure about it. He was a key part of the football team; he was growing closer to Tee and of course Danoom were as strong as ever. Life was good.

John Jameson had been quite shaken by what had happened. He joined a few colleagues for an end-of-term drink, and got thoroughly drunk. He didn't tell anyone of his altercation with Allison. He began to fear it really was more serious than he thought. She was genuinely threatening to spread evil and false rumours about him. He was determined to enjoy his three-week holiday and then formulate a plan on his return to work.

Noom lay back on his bed and started to ponder if Tee really did have a crush on Danai. Was everyone gay? He thought again about his kiss with Danai. He realised he was getting hard and feeling turned on thinking about Tee and Danai as a couple. He decided to shower and jerk off before sleep. He felt guilty and weirded out that he had jerked off, thinking about Tee and Danai together. Teenage life was complicated, but life was good, he thought to himself as he nodded off to sleep.

'Three's A Crowd' – Book Two in the Bangkok Silom International School Series will be released very soon. Make sure you sign up at www.jakeleeauthor.weebly.com for notification of the release date and a free sample of Book Two!

ABOUT THE AUTHOR

Jake Lee spent time at international schools both as a student and as a teacher before deciding to become a writer. Jake lives in Bangkok and considers the city very much his home.

"As an openly gay man, Bangkok is a great city to live. Generally, I have found Thai people to be incredibly accepting. I have never had a situation where I've not felt I could be open and out with a new person. As for my 'Tee' I am sure he is out there somewhere!"

Jake Lee 2023